I0823746

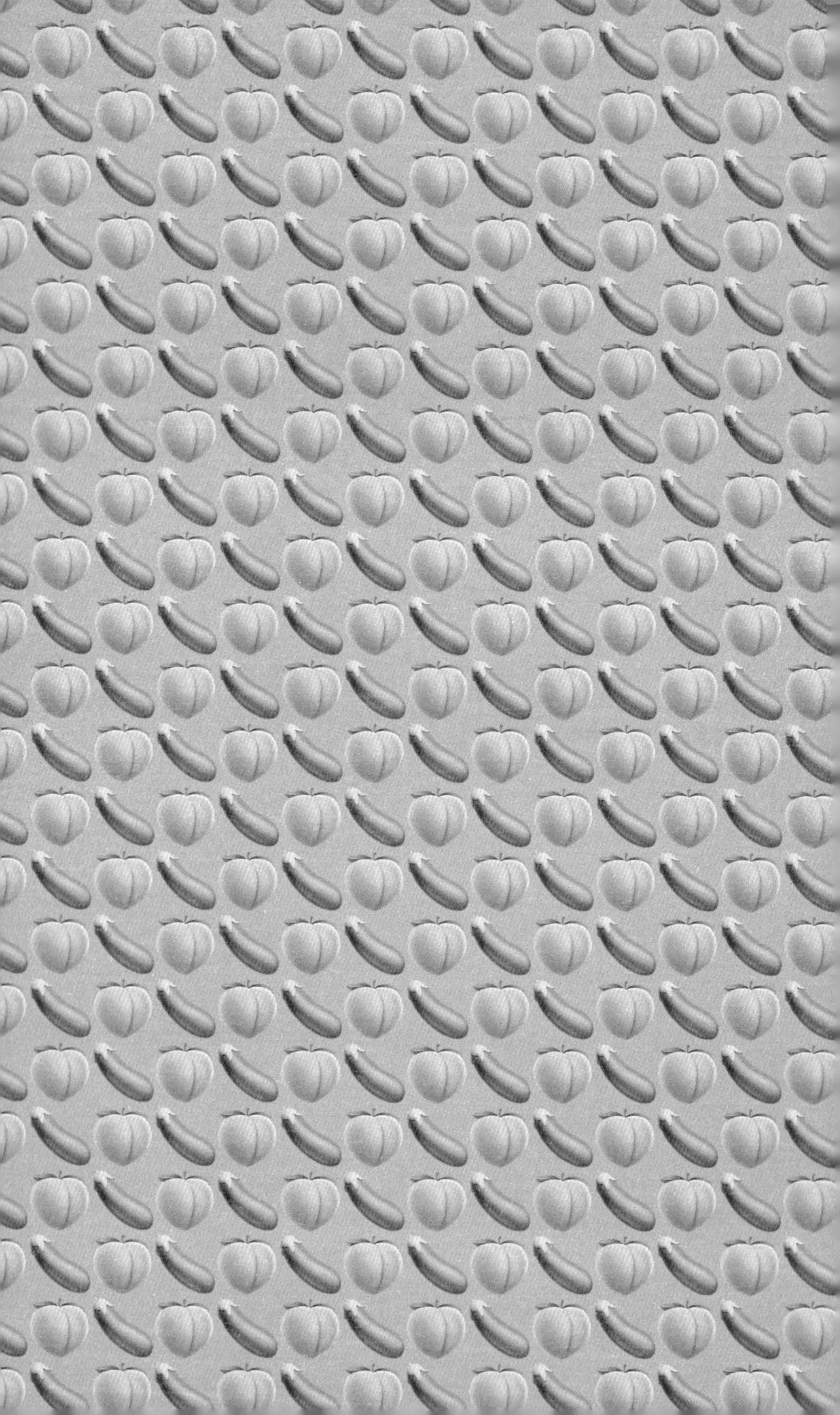

ENJOY YOUR STAY AT *The Shamrock Motel*

ENJOY YOUR STAY AT

ANDREW KAUFMAN

COACH HOUSE BOOKS, TORONTO

first edition

Canada Council for the Arts
Conseil des Arts du Canada
Canada

ONTARIO ARTS COUNCIL
CONSEIL DES ARTS DE L'ONTARIO
an Ontario government agency
un organisme du gouvernement de l'Ontario

Published with the generous assistance of the Canada Council for the Arts and the Ontario Arts Council. Coach House Books also acknowledges the support of the Government of Canada through the Canada Book Fund and the Government of Ontario through the Ontario Book Publishing Tax Credit.

LIBRARY AND ARCHIVES CANADA CATALOGUING IN PUBLICATION

Title: Enjoy your stay at the Shamrock Motel / by Andrew Kaufman.
Names: Kaufman, Andrew, 1968- author
Description: First edition.
Identifiers: Canadiana (print) 20250113988 | Canadiana (ebook) 20250134365 | ISBN 9781552455012 (softcover) | ISBN 9781770568457 (EPUB) | ISBN 9781770568570 (PDF)
Subjects: LCGFT: Novels.
Classification: LCC PS8571.A892 E55 2025 | DDC C813/.6—dc23

Enjoy Your Stay at the Shamrock Motel is available as an ebook: ISBN 978 1 77056 845 7 (EPUB), ISBN 978 1 77056 857 0 (PDF)

Purchase of the print version of this book entitles you to a free digital copy. To claim your ebook of this title, please email sales@chbooks.com with proof of purchase. (Coach House Books reserves the right to terminate the free digital download offer at any time.)

For Shannon

‘The behaviour of a human being in sexual matters is often a prototype for the whole of his other modes of reaction in life.’

– Sigmund Freud,
Sexuality and the Psychology of Love

TABLE OF CONTENTS

Sixteen All-True Facts About the Shamrock Motel

1. The Shamrock Motel doesn't accept reservations.
2. The office doesn't have a computer, wifi, or even a fax machine. Rosemary Liszt, owner/operator of the Shamrock, doesn't believe in cellphones. Cell reception at the Shamrock is intermittent at best. Text messages, when they do arrive, appear in Anishinaabemowin.
3. The office has a landline and you can call it, but your call will go unanswered.
4. There is only one way to get a room at the Shamrock Motel: go into the office, walk across the thin grey carpet, and ask for one.
5. Arriving at the Shamrock isn't a matter of lefts and rights but of mishaps and doubt. Of fate disguised as accidents and accidents disguised as fate. Some are compelled to get into their cars and drive unknown roads until they see the Shamrock's pink-and-green neon sign shining through the darkness. Others stumble upon the Shamrock in the middle of the day, on their way to somewhere else, without any knowledge whatsoever that this was their destination all along. However

you got here, be thankful that you've arrived. A little bit terrified of course, obviously, but grateful that the key in your hand opens a room at the Shamrock Motel.

6. Unless called, guided by an invisible hand, or following directions whispered into your ear, never attempt to find the Shamrock Motel. It won't work. You won't find the Shamrock until your need is overwhelming, until you've been broken into small enough pieces to accept the help the universe is offering.
7. You don't find the Shamrock Motel. The Shamrock Motel finds you.
8. Try not to stare at Rosemary's hair.
9. Under no circumstances should you attempt to request a particular room. Take the room she gives you. Rosemary knows best. You may not like the room. Your experience inside it may – actually, most likely will – change the way you see the world, how you interact with it, and who you are as a person. But trust that Rosemary has selected the right room for you.
10. You don't pick your room at the Shamrock Motel, the room picks you.
11. Room keys accidentally taken by guests can be returned postage-free by dropping them in any Canada Post mailbox. Management is not responsible for any other items guests may unknowingly leave with, including: personal growth, insights into self, awareness of difficult changes you need to make in your life, or expanded awareness of social inequities.
12. Try to remember that the Shamrock Motel is a living thing. The Shamrock isn't just a collection of wood and

plaster, but an idea, an inspiration, a spirit. The Shamrock Motel is an accumulation of all the freedoms previously found there and all the pleasures soon to be discovered. So don't fuck with shit and don't steal the towels.

13. It's up to Rosemary to keep this spirit alive. So don't leave a mess. She's got enough to do without picking up after you.
14. Customer review cards can be found in the top right drawer of the credenza. If you have the time, please rate your experience at the Shamrock Motel on a scale from euphoric to terrifying.
15. The Shamrock is a tiny oasis of permission, a two-acre spiritual preserve that allows people to find their better selves, break patterns, and gain wisdom through fucking. Which, in this day and age, you'd expect would be an easily accomplished task, that there would be government-funded institutions devoted to this activity, YouTube channels and audio books and radio talk shows encouraging and enhancing discourse. But there aren't. There is only the Shamrock Motel.
16. Credit cards are accepted, but cash is preferred.

Pick Me

1.

Derek Wilson is one of sixteen pedestrians stranded by construction at the southeast corner of Bloor and Spadina, waiting for the flagman to turn the sign from Stop to Slow. He watches the woman approach. There are wisps of white running through her dark black shoulder-length hair and her short skirt reveals well-exercised legs, but the most distinguishing characteristic is the men's watch. The watch is large, metallic, and obviously expensive. It doesn't fit with the way she's dressed and yet he can't picture her without it. The watch bounces up and down on her wrist as she gets closer, looking like she knows him, that she's always known him, knows his darkest secret.

'Look me in the eyes,' she says.

He does, briefly. Troubled, unable to sustain the intensity, he looks at the flagman, whose sign still reads Stop. Unable to resist, he looks back at the woman, who looks up from her watch.

'It's time you started giving and not taking.' Her voice is stressed. She believes her message is crucial. She doesn't look crazy. Derek's mouth goes dry and he shifts his weight from his right foot to his left, like a child needing to pee. The flagger turns his sign to Slow. The crowd moves forward, but Derek stays in place, watches the woman cross the street with everybody else. She's already reached the western sidewalk when Derek darts across, trying to catch up, sure she has something more to tell him, an answer to a question he's never realized he needs to ask. But she has a head start, walks quickly, zigzagging around slower-moving pedestrians, and by the time he reaches the west side of Spadina she's out of sight.

Derek keeps walking west on Bloor. He still doesn't see the woman. He calls his wife. She answers on the fourth ring.

'Hey?' Her voice is stressed. It's four-thirty in the afternoon, the middle of May's workday.

'Hey, baby. Can we get dinner tonight?'

'We're still working on the Carrington thing.'

'Please? It's … it's important to me.'

Derek continues walking. The silence continues as well.

'I'll tell you what: if you get a reservation at … What's the place on King? Around the corner?'

'Lagoon?'

'If you get a table for us … What time do they close?'

'Ten.'

'At nine. I'll meet you there and we can have dinner together, and then I'll go back to the office. How does that sound?'

'It sounds great!' Derek says, even though, to him, it only sounds good.

2.

Only three couples remain at their tables when the waitress returns with two cups of black coffee. The white china cups rattle and the coffee splashes but remains within the cups as she sets them on the crisp white tablecloth. May raises the cup to her lips, then takes the linen napkin from her lap, sets it on the table, and slips her phone into the front pocket of her jacket.

'Do you have chocolate cake?' Derek asks.

'We do,' the waitress replies.

'Then chocolate cake, please.'

'Okay. I've gotta get back to the office,' May says.

'Stay for cake? Please?'

'Okay.'

The waitress returns with a slice of chocolate cake featuring alternating layers of icing and crumb, covered with a frosting so thick roofers could use it as tar. He takes a bite: sterling sweetness, a moistness that's practically submissive, chocolate so rich he feels it nibbling at his receding gumline. It's amazing. Everything he wanted. Then his white teeth meet something that isn't food. Taking his napkin from the tabletop, Derek spits out whatever it is, and when he unfolds the white linen he sees a dime, shiny and silver. He's delighted, transported forty-five years backwards, to birthday parties, kids turning eight and nine and ten, at backyard picnic tables and railroad cabooses turned into seating areas, wearing T-shirts without logos and glasses so out of style they've come back in. Forgotten feelings sweep over him: the desire for adventure, indestructible optimism, the certainty that each day will offer the unknown, and that every slice of cake could have money in it.

'What is it?' May asks.

'I got the dime!' Derek holds up the coin the way other men might hold up a fish, and for a moment he feels the drug-like rush of being chosen.

'Well, that's wonderful. I love you.' May collects her briefcase and pushes back her chair.

'You're going?'

'I said I was going to. Are you upset?'

'I just ... '

'What?'

'I wish that you'd choose me over work.'

'But I just did.' May kisses him on the lips, squeezes his shoulder, and makes her way out of the restaurant. Derek watches her walk away as the maître d' rushes toward their table, arriving so quickly that the candle in the centre of the table flickers. Taking a napkin from the unseated table to their right, the maître d' plucks the dime from Derek's fingers.

'My sincere apologies. I'm so sorry, Mr. Wilson. This is a mix-up. It was for another diner. A special request. You understand. We'll get you a new piece immediately, no charge of course.' Gathering up the plate and still holding the dime, the maître d' carries all of it away. Derek sits at the table, looking down. When the new slice of cake arrives, it goes uneaten.

3.

The next morning, a Saturday, Derek fails to sleep in. He makes coffee but doesn't drink it. May is already at work. The house feels abandoned. He gets dressed, drives around, keeps close to Bloor and Spadina, then realizes he's trying to find the woman with the watch. Derek expands his search. He leaves the city, drives through business districts and around cul-de-sacs, finds himself on the highway, compelled to travel on roads he's never heard of, two-lane highways to concession roads and rural routes, as if something is pulling him forward.

The Shamrock Motel comes out of nowhere, sitting between a field of corn and another of cattle. The massive sign features neon tubes sculpted into script promising post-war miracles like colour TV, a swimming pool, and a phone in every room. At the centre of the sign are three neon shamrocks, small, medium, and large, set one inside the other. When the sign's switched on, the shamrocks illuminate in sequence, green then pink then green again, making it look like the shamrock is beating, that the motel is the heart of the world, still pumping, still going strong.

Dust follows Derek's car into the parking lot, gives up the chase, and settles on the pool loungers, the round orange chairs, and the ice machine. He parks, then goes into the office, which is filled with domesticated plants, and walks across the carpet, which is thin and grey. A woman stands behind the counter, watching him carefully, not exactly judging him but doing something close to it, and Derek tries not to stare at her hair. Bright red, curly, falling, perhaps even cascading, her hair sits on her head like a living thing perched there, projecting authority and power like some unholy combination of witch's cat and policeman's service cap. Her posture is mast-straight, although her shoulders are rounded like beach stones, the whisker-like wrinkles at the corners of her eyes giving vague hints, practically gossiping, that this woman may be older than she looks.

Derek brushes his hand through his own hair, which is still blond and parted in the middle, but keeps getting thinner. Suddenly everything about the way he's dressed – the jeans, the zipperless blue hoodie, the high-tops that lack arch support of any kind – seems all wrong.

'Are you still in love with her?' Rosemary watches Derek carefully as he reaches the counter.

'Who?'

'Whoever it is that isn't with you.'

'I don't even know if I'm still happy with her. She never has time for me.' Derek looks at his shoes. His right lace is untied, which is embarrassing, makes him feel like an uncared-for child.

'And that makes you doubt?'

'She never prioritizes me. Or at least I'm never her top priority.'

'Is that what makes you love her? When she makes you her top priority?'

'I don't know.'

'Yes you do.'

'Honestly, I don't.'

'You do. You're just trying to use your relationship to solve an old problem she has nothing to do with.'

'Okay?' Derek rests his hands on the counter.

Rosemary grabs his wrists, holds them with surprising strength, and does not let go. 'This is your last chance. You can turn around right now, get back in your car, and get out of here. No one will know but you and me. You can return to your regular life, unchanged.'

'But I don't want that.'

'Are you sure?'

'That's the opposite of what I want.'

'What do you want?'

'A room?'

'Is that a desire or a question?' Rosemary squeezes harder, causing real pain.

'I want a room. Please?'

'What?'

'A room.'

'What do you want?'

'Give me a goddamn room!'

'That's better. That we can do.' Rosemary turns around and faces the wall, where sixteen keys hang from sixteen hooks. Pausing only briefly, she selects the key for Room 16 and places it on the counter; then a surprisingly small amount of money exchanges hands.

'What now?' Derek asks, and Rosemary pushes the key slightly closer to him.

4.

The door remains unlocked, and Derek moves around the room, trying to find cell reception. There isn't any. There's a rotary phone on the bedside table, and he calls May's number. It takes forever.

'Derek? You okay?' May asks.

'I need you to come here.'

'Where's here?'

'The Shamrock Motel. Room 16.'

'A motel?'

'Yes.'

'I mean, that sounds wonderful, but we're still on the Carrington thing.'

'But it's Saturday.'

'I know. I know. How long are you staying at … '

'The Shamrock Motel. And I guess I don't know.'

'Okay. This is what I can do. Gary's not here so I can't see us going any later than four. If we wrap around four, I'll come out. It's a pretty big if, though … '

'You can't just come?'

'I can't.'

'Please?'

'I'm giving you what I can. Promise. How would I even get there?'

'Put Harriston into your phone, then take Concession No. 4 on your way out of town. After that you just have to drive around a bit. It won't be easy, but you'll find it. I just wish you'd come now. You know?'

'I know. But I'm giving you all I can.'

'Are you?'

'I am, baby. I gotta go. I'll let you know if I can come out.'

'Wait ... ' Derek says, but she's gone. He keeps the receiver against his ear. The rotary phone produces a tone, which Derek listens to for a very long time. He had forgotten that all the phones used to make this sound, that no call ever ended with silence.

5.

Sitting on the bed, knowing he has some time to kill, Derek turns on the TV. He turns it off. He takes a long shower and, when he comes out, May still hasn't arrived, although it's crazy to think she would have. He falls asleep on the bed, instantly, without dreams, for three and a half hours, and when he wakes up his dick is gone, replaced by a long construction-yellow electrical cord with a two-pole, three-wire, twenty-amp black plug at the end of it.

Derek, curious, gets down on his hands and knees. Pausing only slightly, he unplugs the bedside lamp and plugs himself in. The feeling is electric, amazing – it builds and builds and then Derek's entire body shakes as he moans and cums. Sparks fly out of the wall socket. Blue bolts of electricity shoot up the electrical cord and into his body. There's smoke and a loud pop and Derek is thrown backwards, landing on the thin grey carpet.

The power in Room 16 goes out. The power goes out in all sixteen rooms of the Shamrock Motel, but Derek doesn't know this. He's unconscious. When he wakes up, it's dark outside and the power's still off, but his cock is no longer an electrical cord. His original cock has returned. However, something feels different. Derek can't quite figure out what it is. Still filled with curiosity, he lies on his back and pictures the night Stacey McCurry took him to Amberly Beach. Derek gets hard, quickly, and when he cums he shoots out tiny storm clouds. The miniature clouds drift across the room, flashing tiny bolts of lightning and dropping minuscule amounts of rain onto the carpet. A draft pushes the clouds under the door and they're gone.

At first, this makes no sense to Derek. However, when he thinks about it, his relationship with Stacey had been stormy. She'd been overly focused on her academics and could never find enough time for him. He postulates a theory: Does his new cock ejaculate whatever best describes his relationship with whoever's getting him hot? He lies back down to test his theory, thinking about Donna Pascal in the back seat of a 1984 Ford Thunderbird. In seconds he's rock-hard, even though it's his second time, which also seems to be a feature of his new cock. Soon he's close and he shuts his eyes. When he cums, Derek hears a gunshot and smells gunpowder; looking up, he sees a bullet lodged in the stucco ceiling.

This too makes sense. His relationship with Donna had ended badly. He'd demanded that she make him a priority, that they move in together. She'd refused, they fought, and they never spoke again. Although it's preposterous, Derek concludes that his theory is correct: what his new cock ejaculates depends on how he feels about whoever is turning him on.

It is at this moment that the door of the motel room opens and May enters.

'Starting without me?'

Seeing her husband like this turns May on. It's been a while. May puts the chain across the door.

'You weren't kidding about this place being hard to find.' May kicks off her shoes and gets on the bed. After kissing his mouth, briefly, May works her way south like it's February and she's on vacation.

'Shouldn't we ... eat? Aren't ... you ... hungry?' Derek tries to resist her advances, unsure and slightly terrified of what will happen should she make him cum. 'Maybe we could ... Jesus ... that's ... wow... watch TV?' Concerned, Derek finds the strength to jump off the bed.

'Maybe you should watch me?' May stands up and starts removing clothing. Her underthings are black and insanely delicate. Naked, she climbs onto the bed, gets on her hands and knees, and looks over her shoulder.

'Will you fuck me?'

'It's just that ... '

'Please, baby? I know I've been inattentive, but I need it. I need what you have.'

The last of Derek's resistance evaporates. She guides him in. He is neither tender nor delicate.

'I thought you were going to fuck me? I want you to fuck me. Remember how you used to fuck me?'

Promising himself he'll stop before he cums, Derek fucks his wife harder. This proves mutually beneficial. Overwhelmed with pleasure, Derek feels his orgasm building. He knows he should stop, but he doesn't. He doesn't even slow down. Promising himself that he'll pull out before he's even close to cumming, Derek keeps fucking his wife, harder.

'Cum in me!'

'I can't.'

'I want it.'

'You don't understand.'

'Please? God! Please cum in me!'

Derek doesn't stop. He keeps fucking his wife. He feels that he's close, but he doesn't pull out. He cums harder than he ever has before, filling his wife's cunt with flowers. Daisies and daffodils and sprigs of lavender. He shoots bouquets of violets and bunches of lilies. He cums flowers he doesn't even know the names of. There are flowers everywhere. He fills his wife with so many flowers that they flow out of her, onto the bed, and cover the floor. Soon the whole room is filled with flowers, wall to wall, three feet deep.

If the Bear Makes You Happy

1.

Bonnie was introduced to him through Jenny and Howard Stanton. How Bonnie won custody of the Stantons she didn't know – they were definitely her ex-husband's friends. Maybe the Stantons felt sorry for her. Maybe they had a last-minute cancellation. Whatever their motivation, three months after Bonnie left her husband she was invited to the Stantons' cottage for the July long weekend.

Their directions were eccentric, things like 'first left after the big white rock' or 'when the hydro lines switch from the east side of the road to the west, turn right at the willow tree.' Bonnie's new-to-her car, a hastily purchased Pontiac Sunfire, didn't have GPS, and her phone died half an hour into the trip, so there was a lot of trial and error as she travelled from the city. A lot of gravel roads too, potholes she tried to drive around because her ex-husband's mother's good china was still in the trunk, even though she'd tried to drop it off on three separate occasions. Twice she'd even gone to her ex's house at a time and day they'd both agreed on, only to find all the lights off, his car not in the driveway, and the front door going unanswered no matter how many times she knocked.

But even with all that, and the fact that she got lost several times, the effort was worth it. The Stantons' cottage was in the coastal style, on the water and at the top of a long slow roll of rock. Bonnie got out of her car and just stood there, resting on the driver-side door, staring. The view was gorgeous. The end of her marriage had involved a lot of conflict and disappointment and she'd forgotten things could be gorgeous. With a little tug on the shirt sleeve, Jenny pulled Bonnie out of it. Howard laughed, but gently. Bonnie's odd behaviour endeared her to the Stantons, who had a fondness for slightly broken things.

A pitcher of gin and tonics with fresh limes and lots of ice waited inside. Bonnie was the first to arrive. The second round of gin and tonics had been mostly consumed when the Thompsons arrived. David and Alana Thompson, both redheads wearing shorts with pleats, worked in dentistry. The only strange thing about them was how excessively chipper they were. The Jacksons arrived next, a painter and a photographer, who wore black clothing and whispered into each other's ears as if they were lawyer and client.

The Bear was the last to show, big for a brown bear, with thick shiny fur. Standing on his hind legs, he hugged Jenny and Howard, his ears almost scraping the ceiling. He roared a greeting that, although non-semantic, expressed his gratitude for being invited. His claws clicked on the wooden floor as he walked to the windows and took in the view.

At dinner the Bear was seated to Bonnie's right. The meal was salmon, served with the head still on. She watched the Bear from the corner of her eye as he pressed the tail against the plate with his paw, tearing out the flesh with his teeth, his tongue plucking out the eyes like delicacies. He made utensils seem ludicrous. He ate everything, skin and bones, then his long pink tongue licked the fine-white plate clean, while she left the head, the tail, and a tall pile of good bones on her plate. The Bear's zeal and lack of shame made Bonnie want to pick out the salmon's eyes with the tip of a red-painted nail and pop them into her mouth, but she didn't have the nerve.

'Do you want all this?' These were Bonnie's first words to the Bear. He nodded vigorously and she slid her plate over to him.

They spent the rest of the weekend together, but nothing really happened. About a month later they ran into each other in a bookstore on Quebec Street and decided to get a drink.

One thing led to another and there he was in the passenger seat of her car as she drove back to Room 12 at the Shamrock Motel, and the next thing Bonnie knew, she'd fucked a bear.

2.

The next morning Bonnie woke up before the Bear. Her motel room, 12, was filled with his thick, earthy scent. The Bear had been a great lay. She'd spent sixteen years married to a man who equated tenderness with respect. The Bear didn't. Slipping out of bed just before her alarm rang, she showered, dressed, and was bending over to tighten the straps on her shoes when she felt a sharp pain on her back. Her shirt was stuck to her skin. Twisting around, Bonnie looked in the mirror. On each side of her spine were four bright red bloodstains, thin, in lines, all about eight inches long, soaking through her white cotton dress shirt.

Taking her shirt off like it was on fire, twisting her upper body, Bonnie looked over her shoulder and examined her wounds in the mirror above the sink. These were deeper than cuts: they were lacerations. The Bear had played rough, they both had, but he'd shown no desire to harm. Lord knows he'd had numerous opportunities to. No, these eight slashes reflected in the mirror were the Bear's version of raking fingernails down her back, although this did not make Bonnie feel safer. Replaying the night before, Bonnie saw that the reason she hadn't been mauled by a bear was the intensity of delight she'd provoked in him; if she'd been slightly better in bed, she'd be dead.

Most of her wounds Bonnie couldn't reach, but she did what she could with Band-Aids and gauze, then promised her reflection that she'd never do anything so stupid again. Inching the bathroom door open, she looked: the Bear was sleeping. Holding the wire hangers to prevent clanging, Bonnie pulled a second white dress shirt out of the closet. She found her briefcase and keys and wrote a note expressing how wonderful the evening had been and that the door would lock automatically when he closed it behind him.

She was already driving to work when she wondered if the Bear could read.

3.

Three hours later Bonnie entered Boardroom 6 still thinking about the Bear. Distracted, she walked past her usual chair at the back of the room and was forced to take a seat at the front right corner of the table, much closer to Lorraine, her boss. Surprisingly, Bonnie liked her new position very much. Fucking the Bear made her feel like a risk-taker, the kind of woman she imagined she'd be if she hadn't spent so long in a loveless marriage. These feelings influenced her behaviour throughout the meeting, making her more outspoken and direct. It all culminated when she interrupted Lewis Clyde's rambling assessment of a distribution shortfall with a proposed solution. Her idea had merit, and Clyde's quick rejection of it was interrupted by Lorraine herself.

'Are you saying we could just lease out the existing fleet?' Lorraine asked Bonnie.

'I am. It would give us thirty-two more units, all of which we could return to domestic rotation.'

'But what about the Dasia Effect?' Lorraine asked.

'It wouldn't come into effect. The integration wobble is only generated by numbers greater than forty. Which we're safely below at thirty-two.'

'Clyde, is this right?'

'Well, mathematically it could work.' Clyde clenched his yellow teeth.

'Then do it. Next item?'

Near the end of the day, Bonnie had a second victory. She'd shut down her computer and was putting on her running shoes when the phone on her desk rang. There were only three minutes left before the workday ended, which made her suspect it was her ex-husband. She held the receiver away from her face, like an iron that might still be hot.

'Bonnie Greenberg.'

'Do you have any idea what today is?'

'Please don't call me at work.'

'It's the anniversary of our first date.'

'Okay?'

'You forgot that, didn't you?'

'I guess I did, Larry.'

'You've forgotten a lot of things.'

'Not the important ones.'

'You forgot how to love me. That's what you forgot. You know you were never there for me. It was always about you, what you needed.'

This is where, under normal conditions, Bonnie would begin trying to convince Larry that his perspective was misguided. She would use events from their marriage as examples of where her needs became secondary to his. She would speak honestly, sometimes for hours, without getting mad or raising her voice, as she attempted to change Larry's mind. But, having just fucked a bear, she no longer felt the need to do this. For the first time it was clear that this approach had never worked and was never going to.

'That's not the way I see it,' Bonnie said in a firm, confident voice, which was new, which she liked the sound of. 'And you have to get your mother's china out of my trunk or it's going to Goodwill,' she said, and hung up the phone before Larry, who'd already taken a deep breath, could say anything.

4.

That night, Bonnie didn't hurry back to her motel room to read and watch television. She went out for dinner and bought an eighteen-dollar glass of wine. At first, dining alone made her feel peculiar and obvious, but when she realized nobody was even noticing her, the isolation turned into solitude. Driving home, she turned on the radio to a nostalgia station, singing loudly along to songs she remembered from high school. It was dark when Bonnie finally returned to the Shamrock Motel. Parking in her usual spot, she unlocked the door, stepped into Room 12, and was struck by the overpowering scent of bear.

The Bear was still in her room.

Bonnie imagined torn bedsheets, an upended mattress, lamps on their sides. Or was the Bear lying in wait? Somewhere in the dark waiting to attack? You never knew with wild animals. Or did you? She didn't really know. She had so little experience with this kind of thing. Trembling slightly, Bonnie flicked on the overhead light, but the only thing that wasn't where she'd left it was the Bear. He sat in the middle of the room, completely still, his arms wrapped around his body and his snout pressed against his chest.

The moment he saw Bonnie, the Bear threw his paws into the air, pointed the tip of his snout at the stucco ceiling, and gave a growl that expressed his joy at seeing her. Clearly, the Bear had made himself as small and as motionless as possible so that nothing would be broken as he waited for her return. The look on his face sought approval, and Bonnie, moving forward into the room, found herself unable to resist giving it.

Who wouldn't fall in love at least a little bit with a creature willing to work so hard for her love?

5.

They found a safe word, *Yogi*, so Bonnie no longer worried about being mauled. She didn't really want a relationship. She knew it would be much better for her to spend some time, maybe as much as a year, alone after the divorce. Promising herself she'd break things off as soon as the sex fizzled, she continued fucking the Bear all summer long and then into fall. October turned into November, and Bonnie still craved the Bear with a desire she hadn't experienced since first-year university. He lived with her at the motel, but he asked very little of her time or her finances. Plus he was great company – or at least he was always there when she didn't want to be alone.

Learning to live with, even to lean into, transitional things was a skill Bonnie had not expected to learn, at least not at her age. But her relationship with the Bear was, as far as she was concerned, entirely transitional, which was what she loved about it. Same could be said for her continued residency in Room 12 at the Shamrock Motel. Becoming more comfortable with change was giving Bonnie the power to do things at work she'd never have done before. In a shrewd and out-of-character move, she began timing her cigarette breaks to coincide with Lorraine's, and they casually became work friends.

One November morning, cold and crisp, the light flat and blue, Bonnie slept late. She had an important call with the Barcelonians and, in order to make it on time, had to leave Room 12 without showering. The meeting went well, and afterwards, while smoking, Lorraine leaned close to her and sniffed deeply, catching a whiff of something untamed underneath the smell of burning tobacco.

'Who were *you* with last night?' Lorraine's eyebrows were raised.

'Oh. A friend. Just a friend. You know ... '

'A special friend?'

'Okay. Yes.'

'A moose?'

'A bear, actually.'

'A bear! My, my, aren't you full of surprises. Is he ...? Are you ...?'

'We are.'

'Well, if the bear makes you happy ... '

Smiling, Bonnie extinguished her cigarette with a twist of her shoe and went back to her desk without explaining further. Three weeks later, Clyde got fired for losing the Lewisburg account and Bonnie was promoted, becoming Vice-President of Northeastern Redundancies.

Even though the new job was demanding, with longer hours, Bonnie loved it. But she started getting home later and later, and the Bear felt neglected. One weeknight near the end of November, she opened the door to Room 12 and saw that the Bear had become a furry lump on the carpet. He looked up with sad eyes that broke her heart a little bit. She felt guilty about prioritizing work over the Bear, although not enough to make her rework her schedule to get home earlier.

'Hey, why don't we go out this weekend? Somewhere in the city maybe? What about dancing this Friday?' Bonnie asked. The Bear bounded toward her. She put her face deep into his fur as he licked her hand.

'Okay! Okay! Hold on just a minute.' Bonnie went to the bathroom to shower. The Bear waited patiently in bed—it'd been a while, but when Bonnie finally crawled into bed, smelling of soap, her skin still wet, she fell asleep almost instantly.

6.

That Friday, Bonnie got home from work a little late, craving sweatpants, television, and wine, opened the door to Room 12 and saw the Bear sitting on the corner of the bed, his fur freshly washed and combed. The look on the Bear's face, a sad-dog eagerness, the hunch of his shoulders, and the forward lean of his body expressing a great expectancy. This is when Bonnie remembered their date – to go dancing, no less! Her feet hurt. She was exhausted. All day she'd been dealing with other people's problems. Taking a deep breath, she organized a list of excuses in her mind, but when the Bear looked up from the bed with his deep wet eyes, she just couldn't say them.

'All right! Let's go dancing!' Bonnie stripped out of her work clothes, put on a short skirt that maximized the appeal of her legs and a white silk blouse she knew she could dance in.

The Bear was more than happy to drive. He liked driving and rarely got the chance. They parked in a public lot downtown, close to where Bonnie worked. They walked south on Windham Street, with Bonnie leading the way as the year's first snow started falling, white flakes drifting through the windless air, landing in the Bear's fur and melting into nothing.

The windows of the Havana Dance Studio were steamed over, and no amount of glass and wood could prevent the bass-heavy salsa beat from leaking onto the sidewalk. Couples danced inside, the water vapour on the windows turning their motion into streaks of colour. Bonnie held the door open, the Bear bounded inside, and she followed him.

'Good to see you again, Mrs. Lopez. It's been a while.' Sal spoke loudly, to be heard over the music.

'Good to see you too, Sal. But Greenberg. Ms. Greenberg now. Or just Bonnie?'

'Understood.' He gestured for Bonnie to lean closer.

'It's good to see you out, Bonnie. And we're okay with your bear. We don't use the word *predator* here. But if he does go natural, of course you know how to talk him down? Safely? Correct?'

'Naturally.' Bonnie spoke confidently, even though she didn't entirely understand what she was agreeing to, a strategy that was paying off at work. She paid the cover, and when she looked up, the Bear was no longer beside her. Searching the crowd, she found him in the middle of the dance floor, standing high on his hind legs, his arms opened wide, waiting.

'Go get him!' Sal said.

Bonnie rushed out into the middle of the dance floor, where the Bear was waiting. She took his paw and slipped her hand into the fur above his hip, and the Bear became elegant, sweeping her around the floor with long graceful strides. The Bear led beautifully. They slipped past slower-moving couples, the Bear guiding Bonnie toward patches of space that hadn't opened up yet, but did just as they arrived.

She followed the Bear around the dance floor, moving like water, other couples watching them with envy. Closing her eyes, Bonnie pushed her face deep into the Bear's fur, savouring his smell, the feeling of holding and being held. She felt safe, as if nothing in her life was missing, optimistic about the future, until a clumsy waiter dropped a tray of glasses.

The metal tray crashed against the wood floor, sending shards of broken glass and multicoloured cocktails radiating outward, splashing onto Bonnie's bare legs. The Bear, startled, took his paw from Bonnie's waist, let go of her hand, and dropped to all fours. His ears went flat. He pointed his snout at the ceiling and pushed short bursts of air through both nostrils. Then his head fell low and he swung it back and forth, as he slapped the dance floor with his flattened paw. Saliva dripped from the corners of his mouth.

This, Bonnie understood, was going natural.

The couples rushed to get away, but in their panic they moved deeper into the space. The Bear stood between them and the door, growling in a deep voice Bonnie had never heard before that made his claws look sharper. The muscles in his back legs tensed. She did not carry pepper spray in her purse, and the pots and pans in the kitchen were too far away to be clanged together: she had only one thing that she could turn into a weapon.

'I am disappointed in you!' Bonnie stomped her foot. 'Who is this bear? This is not the bear that I know. Where is my bear? The bear that I love?' Bonnie used her deepest voice, gave a firm staccato hand clap, and stomped her foot at the end of each question. The Bear glanced up, looking like a dog caught stealing food, and put his massive head close to the floor. His growling ceased. He took a tentative step toward her.

'Are you gonna be a good bear or a bad bear?'

The Bear lowered his head even more as he took a second small step.

'Because I have love only for the good bear. Which are you?'

Keeping his head low, the Bear took tiny steps toward her. Bonnie crossed her arms. Her feet did not move, and when the Bear reached her, he pushed his snout into the crook of her arm. The Bear's long pink tongue licked her hand. She rubbed behind his ears.

'Good Bear! That's my good bear!'

The crowd parted for Bonnie and the Bear as they walked toward the exit. Sal nodded, impressed, and held the door open for them. The snow was still falling as they walked down Windham Street, large delicate flakes that seemed uninterested in reaching the ground. Bonnie's hand rested in the thick fur at the back of his neck. They walked slowly, strolling, taking their time to get back to the car. Outside Room 12 the Bear waited to be asked in, then he fucked her so hard Bonnie almost believed she loved him back.

The next morning the Bear kept sleeping. His breathing was deep. His heartbeat was slower than normal. She poked the Bear and nothing happened. She shook him and he still didn't respond. Bonnie yelled in his ear, but no matter what she did, he remained sound asleep.

The Bear didn't wake up for the sixteen weeks.

7.

How Bonnie loved sleeping beside the hibernating bear! His body temperature was two degrees cooler than normal, so she could clutch as much of his bulk as her arms allowed, bury her face in his fur, and still remain cool. The Bear never complained and was content to share nothing more intimate than the air they breathed. All he wanted was sleep.

The Bear slept into December and January and February, his sleep getting deeper as the snow did too.

8.

In March the seasonal decrease in Bonnie's serotonin production was exacerbated by how challenging work had become. Office politics and corporate cutbacks increased her workload, tightened her deadlines, and made her co-workers suspicious, tired, and backstabbing. Almost every night she cried in her car on the way home, but she could always count on the Bear being there for her, lying in her bed, ready to be held as she whispered the events of her horrible day into his long pointed ears.

This is how she passed the winter.

9.

One day in the third week of April, Bonnie's cigarette is close to the filter when Lorraine comes out and asks to bum one. She has never been without cigarettes before. Lorraine's clothes are wrinkled. There are deep black circles under her eyes. Her fingers hold the cigarette uncertainly, like tiny birds desperate to land on a branch moving in the wind.

'Are you okay?' Bonnie lights a second cigarette.

'Nothing causes more damage than holding on to something for too long,' Lorraine says, exhaling a long plume of white smoke, which hangs in the still air. They listen to traffic.

'That's good advice,' Bonnie says.

Lorraine looks at her cigarette, the majority of which remains unburnt, then flicks it into the street. Touching Bonnie on the shoulder lightly and briefly, she goes inside.

Lorraine resigns later that day and Bonnie never sees her again.

10.

That night Bonnie doesn't rush home. She stays in the office, watching amateur critics on YouTube review movies she loved in high school. She takes a convoluted route on her way home, travelling concession roads, rolling down her windows, and breathing in the smell of fresh spring mud. Shortly after midnight, she pulls over to the side of the road. Her foot remains on the brake. She doesn't put the car into park or turn off the engine. She closes her eyes, stays perfectly still, then lifts her foot off the brake and makes a U-turn on the gravel road. Driving quickly, in the direction she has just come from, Bonnie returns to the city, straight to the house Larry has rented. The clock on the dashboard says 1:17 when she parks behind his car in the driveway. All the lights are off. Getting out, Bonnie opens the trunk and makes three trips, setting all of Larry's mother's dishware on the top step in front of his house. She rings the doorbell six or seven times, then gets back into her car. She has already reversed out of the driveway by the time the front door opens.

She doesn't look back.

When Bonnie parks in front of Room 12, only the lights in Room 9 and Room 14 are on. She sits behind the wheel of her car, listening to the sounds of the motel, which have become familiar: the hum of the single street light watching over the parking lot, ice dropping in the ice machine, the Bear snoring. She goes inside and sits on the edge of the bed, watching the Bear like he's television, envious of his stillness. The sun is starting to rise when his right shoulder twitches. He yawns. Bonnie pushes her face deep into his thick black fur and listens to his heartbeat; all winter, his heart has been beating so slowly, but now it's beating quickly again.

Crawling on top of the Bear, Bonnie puts her face close to his. She wants to be the first thing he sees. She calls in sick to work. Finally, just after noon, the Bear opens his eyes. Seeing Bonnie, he pulls up his lips and exposes his teeth in a gesture that looks like a snarl but that she recognizes as his closest approximation of a smile. But Bonnie's face remains blank. She flips through feelings like someone in a motel room watching TV. Joyful, weepy, relieved: none of them feels right. She doesn't want to admit that the difference between loving a sleeping bear and one who's awake is vast, but there it is, in her heart.

All the Bear sees is her disappointment.

11.

For the next thirteen weeks, they try to stay together, but they both know it's over, that they're holding on to something too long and causing damage to each other. On what will turn out to be the hottest day in August, Bonnie sits on the corner of the queen-sized bed and the Bear sits beside her. The sun is just beginning to rise. She doesn't know why this is the day she can do it. She doesn't know what has changed. She holds his paws and they stay still, then fuck in a sad and delicate way. When he cums, the Bear releases a mournful growl, which conveys several things: that they shouldn't discount what they had because it's over, that the merits of sadness must be embraced on equal terms with those of joy, that he wants her to never forget that he loved her, which is the greatest thing living creatures can do with the brief moments they're given to exist.

It's a lot to put in a growl, but the Bear pulls it off.

Then the Bear gets out of bed, stands on his hind legs, and opens his arms. They hug. She doubts she will ever be hugged like this again. Dropping to all fours, the Bear waits for Bonnie to open the door, and when she does he lopes into the parking lot. It's early morning. The sun is just about to clear the trees. The street light turns off as he passes underneath it. She's surprised by how fast he can run. He is already across the highway, about to go into the forest. He doesn't look back. Twenty minutes later, Bonnie has everything loaded into her car and stands in the office, finally ready to check out of the Shamrock Motel.

Kindling

The dining-room chair is part of Julie's inheritance, handmade by her grandfather, a well-crafted but well-used antique, a veteran of overweight uncles and late-night life-changing decisions. Julie drags it to the top of the stairs, steps on the seat, finds her balance, raises her hands over her head, and removes the smoke detector's white cover. The nine-volt battery dangles by its positive and negative connections. Putting all her weight on her right leg, Julie stretches her arm and, as her fingertips touch the battery, the chair leg snaps.

Julie falls to the right. The chair isn't so lucky. She watches it crash down the steps, the seat separating from the apron, the front left leg taking chunks out of the drywall, the spindles set free as the top rail splinters. When the chair reaches the bottom, it's no longer a chair – it's kindling. Still on the floor, Julie looks up, sees the exposed innards of the smoke detector, the battery hanging like an eyeball out of its socket.

Instead of getting another chair, Julie opens the bottle of wine they've been saving. It's almost four in the afternoon when she takes her wineglass into the backyard, drags a lawn chair out of the shade, pulls up her skirt, and opens her legs, wide, so the hot afternoon sun can reach all of her. Three glasses later, her husband gets home: no dinner, the house a mess.

The missing chair goes unnoticed. Over the next three weeks, Brian doesn't notice her new underwear, that she's stopped eating meat and started making their bed the moment she gets out of it. He doesn't notice how quickly she responds to Clark's texts, or that she's started replying even after midnight, when she should be in bed but is still on the couch.

There's no way Brian could know that when Clark approaches at work, as he's been doing more and more since they're started working on the Mendelson file, she no longer backs away. She hasn't mentioned this to Brian. She's also remained silent about how much harder it's getting not to take a step toward Clark, that the only things stopping her are her threadbare loyalty to Brian and how they're usually surrounded by co-workers.

Five weeks after the chair shatters, Julie and Brian are driving to Chesley, a nowhere village in the middle of nothing, to visit his sister's newborn daughter. Julie's driving. Brian's sleeping. The phone suggests going left, but Julie goes straight. Three rural routes later, she turns right. The phone is turned off. She doesn't know what she's doing. Nothing like this has ever happened before; it's like someone's whispering directions to her at every corner. The road becomes gravel, and then, after cresting a hill, she sees the Shamrock Motel, the windows of all sixteen rooms reflecting the sun.

Julie turns in but stops before she enters the parking lot. Brian continues sleeping. Julie closes her eyes and tries to focus on love and commitment and getting through the bad times and persevering: all she sees is the chair tumbling down, smashing into kindling. Her eyes are still closed as she reverses back onto the road and turns around. In sixteen minutes she reaches her sister-in-law's and parks on the street. Brian is still asleep. Julie doesn't wake him, doesn't look back as she walks across the front yard, collecting twigs and fallen branches that she'll later use to build a fire.

All Sixteen Rooms of the Shamrock Motel, Briefly Described

Every room at the Shamrock Motel offers 324 square feet, a three-piece bathroom, a queen-sized bed, cable colour television, a credenza, a closet, six wooden hangers, two large towels, sheets, a flower-print bedspread, a spare blanket, and something else that is absolutely and completely intangible. It's this intangible part – some call it an energy, others a spirit, and some truly believe each room is a living, organic thing – that makes the Shamrock different from every other motel in the world.

The Shamrock Motel has sixteen rooms and an infinite number of stays. No two nights at the Shamrock Motel have ever been the same. Even if two people spent consecutive nights in the same room, their stays would be different. Just like no two children have exactly the same parents, no guest experiences the same stay. This is because the Shamrock is as affected by the people staying in her rooms as they are by her. A partial list of the things a typical guest brings into whichever room Rosemary selects includes: their experience of love and sex, their parents' experience with love and sex, their emotional baggage, their parents' emotional baggage, the successes of their past relationship, the failures of their past relationships, the degree to which their true selves fit into current cultural norms, the amount of shame produced by their inability to fit into cultural norms, the state of their current relationship, the state of their current relationship last week, the entire backstory of their current relationship and how they feel about themselves and their partners as they walk through the door of their motel room.

Now multiply all of that by the number of people staying in the room and you're beginning to see why no two stays at the Shamrock have ever been the same and no two ever will be.

Room 12, as usual, being the exception that proves the rule.

However, with all that being said, there are general ideas and currents – call them themes if you need to – working within each of the Shamrock's sixteen rooms. This is why the hardest part of Rosemary's job isn't the laundry, or the repairs, or finding the money to keep paying the bills and buying new sheets: it's selecting the right room for every guest. This a very tricky matter. Putting a guest in the wrong room can have disastrous results.

It has in the past. Rosemary has an incredibly short amount of time to make her selection, and all she has to work with is the way they pull into the parking lot and exit their vehicles, what their body language says as they walk across the thin grey carpet from the office door to the counter. Obviously, she runs on instinct. Rosemary's greatest skill is trusting herself to select the perfect room for every guest.

Or at least the room they deserve.

Room 1

Guests staying in Room 1 will suddenly be able to see an inner strength and depth of character they didn't know they had – or, as is more commonly the case, were afraid to discover.

It's also the only room with a mirror on the ceiling, which may or may not be coincidental.

Room 2

Room 2 is best not spoken of.

Room 3

You know the thing that you're most proud of? The thing you're sure makes you a good person? That defines you? It has to go. Right now, it has to go, and Room 3 is here to help.

Room 4

Room 4 has not been rented out for three years, four months, and sixteen days. No one, not even Rosemary, has gone inside Room 4 in all that time, not since the horrible thing happened. Every once in a while, when Rosemary is feeling either exceptionally strong or unbelievably sad, she'll stand in front of the door to Room 4 and put all ten of her fingertips against the thin white-painted wood.

Sometimes, when her grief is so overwhelming it's like an anchor pulling her down through pitch-black water, she puts her ear against the wooden door. She stands there, neglecting the laundry that has to be done, the acres of carpet that need to be vacuumed, the pool water that needs to be skimmed, listening. But all she ever hears is silence.

Room 5

In Room 5 a man once dreamed that he lived on the east coast and became convinced that something bad would happen to his daughter if he looked away from her, even for an instant. So he kept a close eye on her. He went without sleep so he could watch her sleep. He got a job at her school so he could watch her while she was in class. While he was watching her, an asteroid struck the earth at the exact midpoint of the Atlantic Ocean, and as the resulting tsunami swept both him and his daughter away, the man kept watching her, convinced that his gaze was more powerful than the wave, that he could still keep her safe.

When the dreamer woke up, he called his daughter.

'Hello?' she asked.

'It's me. It's Dad.'

'Okay.'

'Are you okay?'

'Yes. I am. I'm totally okay. I'm better than okay. Dad, I'm doing well. I have been for years,' she said, her tone of voice loving but also frustrated. Her dad had been asking her this question for as long as she could remember and, having just had a dream where she was able to perfectly articulate everything she ever wanted to say but didn't know how, she continued.

'You have to stop asking me this. Because it makes me feel like you're not listening to me. Even worse, it feels like you don't believe me. Or at the very least don't trust me to tell you the truth.

'And yes, are there some times when I'm not okay? There are. For sure. But I can handle them. You can support me. You can encourage me. But I have to fix my own problems. That's just the way it is.'

There was a silence, which the man finally broke.

'Okay. I'm sorry. I love you,' he said.

'I love you too.'

The call was ended. The man showered and dressed and returned the room key and drove away without looking back. Ever since this moment, anyone staying in Room 5 will have the power to accept that their worst fear is held only for their own benefit.

Room 6

It doesn't matter which mirror you look in while staying in Room 6 – the one above the sink, the surface of a freshly poured cup of coffee, the face of your partner – you will find something unexpected, potentially repulsive, and absolutely freeing staring back at you.

Room 7

Room 7 gives the answer, but not the question.

Room 8

Room 8 makes you stop lying to yourself. What you do with this power is completely up to you.

Room 9

Room 9 doesn't give a fuck.

Room 10

You will not like Room 10. You will be uncomfortable in it. You will wish that Rosemary had given you the key for any other room at the Shamrock Motel. But there is no denying that, by the time you leave it, you'll realize that your biggest fear is your secret wish.

Room 11

Room 11 will treat you like your best friend would. So be really sure about who your best friend is before spending the night in Room 11.

Room 12

This is the only room at the Shamrock available for rent on a long-term basis. The longest stay was two years and thirteen days. The shortest stay was twenty-seven minutes. Although the possibility of a long-term rental at the Shamrock has never been advertised and is rarely spoken of, the longest period between occupants so far has been forty-seven minutes.

It's these forty-seven minutes that give Rosemary Liszt the faith she needs. With little financial return and very long hours, especially now that she's on her own, there are many reasons why Rosemary should simply shut down the Shamrock Motel for good.

But she doesn't. She keeps believing in what she's doing. It's these forty-seven minutes that allow her to do it, that show her that she doesn't really own the Shamrock Motel, that the Shamrock Motel is owned and operated by forces larger than herself, larger than all of us put together.

Room 13

Don't stay in Room 13. If Rosemary offers this room, you need to back away slowly and reassess every decision you've ever made.

Room 14

Room 14 has been undergoing renovations since 1987.

Room 15

Room 15 is stronger than you are. It will shatter you, disassemble you into your smallest parts like a soldier taking apart their weapon, like a child crumbling a cookie, then let your greatest fear rebuild you into something new, remarkable, and previously inconceivable.

It's also the only room that comes with bathrobes.

Room 16

Room 16 reminds you that the problem isn't absence or disappearance but retrieval. That whatever has gone missing – keys, joy, love, hope – continues to exist.

You've just forgotten where you put it.

Sally Tells the Time

1.

They're in Room 887 of the Royal York Hotel, not a suite, but at least a king with a decent view of Union Station and a slice of the CN Tower if she cranes her neck to the right. Still in bed, covered by a single sheet of high-thread-count white cotton, Sally Temple watches one of her favourites eliminate his nakedness with layers of cotton and linen and wool. A long time ago, when she first started, Sally would have slipped out of bed and gotten dressed with him, an attempt to provide a note of true domesticity to the experience. But nobody wanted that. That was the opposite of what they wanted; her clients have no desire to see her as someone whose shift is over. They want to think of her as one of the hotel's amenities, like the masseuse or room service. So now she stays in bed, naked, watching as they dress and leave, wearing nothing but the wisps of white in her dark black hair and a single sheet of high-thread-count cotton.

This one, whom she knows as Jesse, is a favourite. Nothing fancy, hard and fast, and when he wants something weird he just asks for it, treats her like a chef at a nice restaurant being asked by a regular for something off-menu. Plus his body is amazing. But something about the lighting, maybe his position in the room, makes her notice imperfections in his body, things she never noticed until he starts covering them up. Weird burn marks on his hands as he buttons up his shirt. An appendectomy scar on his right side as he tucks shirttails into his pants. The remnants of some kind of old injury, probably sports-related, on his feet as he pulls up dark black socks. Folding a blue-and-green-striped tie until it fits into his suit pocket, Jesse stands with his shoulders back in the middle of the room. She knows he's trying to figure out if he should kiss her goodbye, navigating the boundaries between professional and personal. Sally takes advantage of his silence.

'Is this real to you?' Sally asks.

'What do you mean?' Jesse pats the pockets of his jacket, feeling the square of his wallet, the rectangle of his phone, the points of his keys.

'What just happened here. Is it real to you?'

Jesse is a regular, a predictable part of her income. This is a big risk, how far she's going off script, but lately Sally's been noticing something in the pace of his redressing and retreat. A motivating factor that isn't guilt, or the fear of being caught, but a wish to erode the validity of what just transpired, to negate the authenticity – not of just the fucking but of everything that comes with it. Sally wonders if this desire is something new, but she suspects it's always been there, that the only new thing is that she's started seeing it.

'That's a weird question,' he says.

'But we ... you ... have had some breakthroughs. Today even. And larger ones in the past. No?' Sally sits up in bed. The cotton sheet falls. It doesn't attract Jesse's attention.

'I can't deny that.'

'You discovered things about yourself. By fucking me? What we just explored. Did you not?'

'Yes. I did.'

'And yet I feel like you're not treating it as real. That this experience will evaporate as soon as you get out of this room, in the elevator down to the lobby. Because you gave me money it means you don't have to take it seriously, that the sex, the experience, was just pretend. An exhibition game? Something that has no connection to your life, no weight in the real world. And you'd never do that to your shrink. You give your psychiatrist money, she charges a fee, literally charges you by the hour, just like me. You'd never use her fee to disavow a breakthrough you had in there. So what's the difference?'

The room is quiet. Traffic moves slowly down Front Street. A room-service cart is pushed down the hallway, empty plates and empty glasses clinking together. Jesse sits on the edge of the bed.

'What are you looking for? What do you need me to say?' he asks.

'It's just that you come into this room weak and scared and powerless. And you leave with confidence and ... joy? Reborn? A little bit anyway. You're like a whole new person. You know? If your therapist effected change like that, would you deny its authenticity?'

'My therapist doesn't use a pseudonym.'

'You're using one too.'

'My therapist doesn't work out of a hotel room.'

'Maybe she should try it.'

'Are you looking for redemption? Do you feel bad about your work? Guilty?'

'No. Not really.'

'Then what are you looking for?'

'Acknowledgement? Validation?'

'Well, then you may have picked the wrong line of work.' Jesse stands up, briefly looks around the room for something forgotten, doesn't see anything. Nodding toward the envelope left by the television, he walks briskly across the carpet toward the door and doesn't turn around. A mechanism decelerates the door's movement, so he's already at the elevator by the time it closes completely.

2.

It isn't until Sally's out of the shower that she hears the ticking. The traffic on Front Street is now gridlocked, and in the moment between the sound of motion disappearing and the honking starting, the room is quiet enough to hear it. Tracking the sound, Sally pushes the bedside table out of the way and sees it on the thick beige carpeting. The watch has a golden face and a thick leather strap. It looks expensive, but more than that it looks like an antique, an heirloom, something handed down from generation to generation.

Sixteen minutes pass. He hasn't returned. When she's fully dressed, he still hasn't come back. Sally tucks the envelope into her purse and then, the last thing she does before leaving the room, straps the watch onto her wrist.

3.

The concierge, who took notice of her when she arrived, is looking at her again as Sally moves across the lobby, head held high, heels click-clacking, trying to draw the right amount of attention to herself – enough but not too much. Wanting to present a nonchalance, that she belongs in this space, Sally looks at the golden watch on her wrist – it's stopped ticking. The watch's hands are frozen, which makes Sally freeze too. She fiddles with the knobs, shakes her wrist and raises the watch to her ear, listens for a ticking like a paramedic at a crime scene, but the watch has no pulse.

The disappointment is strong. That she already feels attached to a material object in her possession for under an hour is also confusing. There are other feelings too, even stronger ones, but slippery, hard to define – like she's been put on pause, or in parentheses, as if the opening bracket appeared unnoticed back in the hotel room and now she's living inside a different context, waiting for explanation or clarification, so the closing bracket will appear.

'Can I help you?' the concierge asks, his appearance sudden, so close to Sally that his theatrically thick black moustache is practically sweeping her shoulder.

'My watch has stopped,' Sally says.

'That's too bad. It's a very nice watch. Should I recommend someone to repair?' he says, sincere, even sad for her, the timepiece's obvious expense granting her permission to be in his lobby.

'Next time,' Sally says.

They both nod. She walks toward the lobby door, which the concierge holds open for her.

4.

Four orange-coloured taxis wait outside the Royal York Hotel, lined up like produce at a supermarket. A cabbie smiles and opens the back door, but Sally shakes her head. The cab is too small – she could cram herself into the back seat but she'd have to leave behind the expansiveness she's feeling. Hands in her pockets, taking elongated steps that at a different time of day would mark her as drunk, Sally walks for two and a half hours and only makes it as far as Matt Cohen Park, at the corner of Spadina and Bloor. Sitting on public art, a giant-sized stack of dominoes, Sally faces the 7-Eleven. She's been there, making eye contact with no one, less than five minutes when he sits down beside her.

'That's a nice watch,' he says with a flick of his hair.

Sally says nothing. She doesn't even turn to look at him, keeps her eyes forward, seeing everything she needs to in her peripheral vision. The kid has a sharp nose, cheekbones a sun could set behind, and deep-set blue eyes. She can tell that ten or so years ago he would have been irresistible. But now his brown hair is a little dirtier, thinner. That after so many performances, his easy smile is coming off as rehearsed. Sally knows his type. With a quick estimate she puts him at 18 per cent less pretty than he used to be, resulting in a 35 per cent reduction in charm. A fact he either hasn't noticed or can't accept.

Sally doesn't look at her broken watch. She looks at him, briefly flattered, then touches his shoulder, lightly, with a maternal pat.

'Time you settled down,' Sally says. 'It may already be too late.'

The response is unexpected. He's shocked, like he's just fallen into a winter stream and can only think about how cold the water is, not how he should be trying to get out of it.

'You ... you ... bitch!'

'That doesn't make it untrue.'

He looks away first. Standing, he rushes east down Bloor Street. Sally doesn't bother watching him go. She's watching a group of pedestrians waiting to cross Spadina, held up by construction. She knows the time for each of them. That it's you'll-never-get-your-father's-approval-so-stop-trying o'clock for the man with the grey at his temples. Admit-you're-with-her-for-her-father's-money o'clock to the man in the long beige trench coat. Go-back-to-university o'clock for the late-twenties in Air Jordans and a guitar strapped to her back.

She knows what time it is for everyone. Just by looking at them, watching the way they walk, how they hold their bodies inside their clothing, if they move or fail to move their hands. There are maybe twenty people in view, men and women, rich and poor; for the first time in her life, Sally knows not only how she would counsel them, how she would inch out their fears, help them put courage and strength in that space, but that she's right. That she could help each of them. Every ounce of doubt has been burned away like dew in the sun.

Without looking at the face, Sally raises the watch to her ear. But there is no ticking. When she looks at the hands they remain still.

5.

The watch remains both broken and on Sally's wrist. She wears it at home, out with friends, regardless of her clients' preference. The watch leaves her wrist only when she showers, a time that grows briefer every day. After turning off the water, the first thing Sally reaches for isn't a towel, but the watch.

Five weeks and three days after receiving the watch, Sally arrives at the Shamrock Motel. In past visits it's taken her hours to find the Shamrock, but this time she finds it easily, parks beside the swimming pool forty-five minutes ahead of schedule. The black leather interior of her Saab 900 quickly overheats in the afternoon sun. Sunlight bounces off the surface of the pool water. Leaving her keys in the ignition, Sally exits her vehicle and lies in one of the loungers circling the pool. Her eyes close. She drifts close to sleep, although she's prevented from getting there when someone takes the lounger to her right. Sally's annoyed – twelve other loungers circle the pool, all of them empty. Why has he taken the one right beside her? It doesn't make any sense. But his voice is beautiful, deep and calming, and somehow familiar, and she opens her eyes.

'Sorry to be so forward, but there's no one else around. No one will see us,' Jesse says.

'Well, isn't this a pleasant surprise,' Sally says.

'Glad that you feel that way. Enjoying the day?'

'So beautiful.' Sally looks up at the sky, then back at Jesse. The sunlight brings out the grey in his hair. She's never noticed he has so much of it.

'Listen, I think I was wrong earlier,' Jesse says.

'About what?'

'You haven't picked the wrong line of work. It's me – it's us who aren't seeing it right.'

'Us?'

'The three of me.'

Several moments pass. Tears pool in Sally's eyes in a most uncharacteristic way. They both look up at the sky, where large birds ride on the wind, black silhouettes against the sun.

'That's a beautiful watch,' Jesse says eventually.

'You like it? One of my clients left it behind. I'm not sure if it was intentional or not. A gift or just forgetfulness.'

'Sometimes they're the same thing.'

'True. I love it. It doesn't work, though.'

'May I?'

'Please.'

Jesse's long elegant fingers reach out and touch the jut, caress the crown, loop the bezel. He opens the pusher and pushes it back in, traces her wrist from the buckle, over the face, with his thumb. His index finger circles the dial, counter-clockwise, slowly, touching the face lightly, until Sally cums. Afterwards they lie on their loungers, watching the pool water sparkle. They stay this way for longer than either of them anticipated.

‘What time is it now?’ Jesse asks.

‘Time you got home,’ Sally says.

Jesse nods. He gets off the pool lounger, looks up at the sky, and ascends. Sally watches him get smaller as he continues going upward. When he disappears, Sally pulls out the crown and sets the hands to the proper time. As she anticipated, as she knew was going to happen, as soon as she pushes the crown back, her watch ticks and ticks and ticks.

See You Next Tuesday

Obviously, they aren't fighting about the spiral ham.

Benjamin, Benny to his friends, a late-thirties graphic designer now vice-president at Looking Good Designs, who's doing his best to learn to love golf, distinctly remembers telling Sarah to pack the fucking ham. Sarah doesn't remember this at all. Sarah, who manages a marketing division of eighty employees and rarely if ever loses track of any details of any kind, who does crossword puzzles as a form of relaxation, wonders why she'd be responsible for the spiral ham when he packed everything else from the refrigerator and put in it his cooler, his fucking Tundra 210 Hard Cooler that cost 1,200 fucking dollars.

They're not fighting about the phone call Sarah took in the driveway even though everything was already packed – except, it seems, the ham – spending sixteen minutes micromanaging some weepy subordinate over an insignificant work-related detail. They're not fighting about having her parents standing at the top of the driveway the whole time, watching, with the kids, not knowing if they should stay or go, awkwardly waiting for them to leave. They're not fighting about how they should have been on the road at eleven and they weren't even in the car until almost noon, or the $80,000 above asking that Sarah bid on their house, or that the font on their wedding invitations was Garamond – Garamond! Or that he'd proposed before he'd bought the ring.

They're fighting about who got them lost: Benny's driving, so the responsibility ultimately lies with him, but it was Sarah's suggestion to turn onto Perth Concession Road No. 178 for no apparent reason. The silence – enduring, uncomfortable, and utterly familiar – gets louder, practically drowns out the sound of the tires on the gravel road, until they crest a hill and see a motel, a little rundown, conspicuously out of place, and kinda adorable.

'If you weren't such a sad pathetic asshole I'd let you take me in there and have me nine ways from Sunday,' Sarah says.

'Bullshit.'

'Fuck you.'

'Absolutely bullshit.'

'It. Isn't.'

'Bullshit!'

'Then go in ... '

'What?'

'You heard me. If you're so sure. Pull in.'

'Fine!'

Benny pulls in and parks beside the swimming pool but keeps the engine running.

Rosemary stands by the office door, looking out at a midnight-black Mercedes-Benz E-Class idling by the swimming pool.

When the engine is finally shut off, she rushes behind the counter. The husband comes in first, his expensive haircut leading the way; he's a little overweight but well-dressed. He fails to hold the door open for his wife, but it's all right: she doesn't seem to notice this quiet lack of empathy, or at the very least didn't expect it from him. The two of them stand at the edge of the room, backs to the wall, taking everything in, appraising it, looking for weakness that can be exploited with the practised eye of management. Then, as if hearing a gunshot, they race toward the counter like athletes competing for gold, arriving in what would surely be a photo finish.

'We'd like a room,' the husband says.

'Do have any king beds?' the wife says.

'King? A queen will be fine. We want a queen.'

'No, a king.'

'Why are you insisting on a king?'

'I'm not insisting. I'm just – '

'Are you afraid of me? Or just need your own space? Want to stay as far away from me as possible?'

' – asking. It'd be nice if you'd let me finish a thought.'

'No vacancies,' Rosemary says.

'What?'

'Pardon?'

'There aren't any rooms available. We're full up. Sorry.'

They both turn and look out the window at the parking lot, where there are far fewer cars than rooms. Their bodies move in sync, like pairs figure skaters as they look back at Rosemary.

'The sign doesn't say that,' Sarah says.

'That's right. The sign says VACANCIES.'

Rosemary turns around. There's a bank of switches at shoulder height on the wall behind her. She flicks the second switch from the left. Outside, on the sign, the NO in front of VACANCIES becomes illuminated.

'You expect us to believe that?' she asks.

'Just 'cause you flicked a switch?' he says.

'That you don't have any rooms?'

'Not one single room?'

Rosemary says nothing, but her smile becomes excessively broad. No matter what question they ask or how loudly they ask it, Rosemary remains mute, the smile on her face never wavering, or shrinking, or changed in any way by their arguments or persistence.

Ben and Sarah look straight ahead as they pull back onto the road. Gravel strikes the wheel well of the midnight-black Mercedes-Benz E-Class. They don't slow down. They drive quickly, in anger, without passing any other cars or trucks or farm equipment. Neither speaks, although the silence has changed, become shared, lost its tension. Just before the motel goes out of sight, they both look back – Sarah over her shoulder and Benny in the rear-view mirror.

'Can you believe it?' Sarah asks.

'Just fucking smiling like that,' Benny replies.

'I hope she likes one-star reviews.'

'Everywhere.'

'Right?'

'What a bitch!' Sarah says.

'What a ... ' Benny stops himself from saying it.

'You can say it.'

'I can't!'

'Say it!'

'Really?'

'I want you to say it!'

'C.U.N.T.!'

'Say it! Just fucking say it, Benny!'

'Cunt! What a fucking cunt!'

'Such a cunt!'

'Cunty cunty cunt!'

'You got that right.'

They keep driving. The silence continues to be all the things it wasn't before. Before they even know it, they've found the main road. A sign proclaims that Clifford, their destination, is only twenty-four kilometres away. Even after all that, they'll arrive on time. As they pass the population sign and drive down the main street of Clifford, they're holding hands.

Serial Monogamist

1.

I used to believe that love lasted forever, like a tattoo; that once cajoled into existence, love could never be destroyed. I believed that love could be ignored, tamed, turned invisible, neutered, that the circumstances between two people could change so drastically that love would become inactive, inert, losing its context and its intensity. But I did not believe that love could be eliminated – until I spent a night at the Shamrock Motel.

My name is Justin Scott Lewis. I have been in love since I was sixteen. Not with the same person, but with numerous people, one right after the other, without gaps. I loved each of them, but when each love lost its lustre, someone new started glowing, and before I knew it, I was in love with them.

However, the love I had with the previous partner never went away. Not completely. Not with me.

No one would vote me the world's best boyfriend, but I try, and on Saturday August 21, I agreed to drive my girlfriend at the time, Angela, to an antique market. A glorified garage sale, if you ask me, the market was being held in Hanover, a quaint small town like all those quaint small towns in Southwestern Ontario that you're happy to visit for the afternoon but don't understand how anyone could live there. We weren't in a hurry, so I took the scenic route, drove unpaved roads, with the windows down, our tires kicking up a trail of dust, as if the gravel-roads ghost was rising toward its heavenly reward.

My plan was to wait until after dinner, to find a nice spot by the river – these quaint small towns always have a river – but it was the perfect day, the perfect time, so I pulled over, took the box out of my pocket, and opened it, exposing the diamond ring inside.

'Will you marry me?' I asked.

Angela paused. The pause continued. I had not expected her to pause at all.

'I will, but on one condition,' she said.

'Yes?'

'Answer me this: Where does love begin and end?' Angela had pulled her black hair into a ponytail that sat on the top of her head. Wind came in through the window, pulling out strands of her hair, whipped them around, looking like ink falling in water. She waited for me to answer. I didn't. I didn't have an answer. This was not the type of question I had an answer for. At my core I am a very shallow man. I'm nothing fancy – I thought that was what Angela liked about me. It was certainly what I liked about her.

Handing Angela the box, which she took, although the ring stayed inside and not on her finger, I started the engine and pulled back onto the two-lane gravel road. It was an attempt to avoid having to answer, or at least to buy me some time, but Angela was not so easily distracted.

'Tell me what you think! Not when or how or why – but where?' She looked over from the passenger seat, closed the box. Her serious eyes were focused on me, demanding at the very least an opinion.

'Not metaphorically – literally,' she continued. 'Inside brain cells? In the gaps spanned by dopamine pathways? By the other person's presence provoking – or failing to provoke – oxytocin, serotonin, and phenylethylamine? Is love even capable of confining itself to a single time and place? Are we sure that love begins and ends?'

Angela stared at me, waiting for my response. But I didn't have one.

'Say something!'

I remained mute, although I put a very serious expression on my face, making it seem like I was deep in thought, that the wheels were turning. This is when a miracle happened: we crested a hill and a roadside motel came into view. A single storey, pleasantly rundown, the sign out front proclaiming it to be the Shamrock Motel. I felt lucky.

For as long as I've known Angela, she's had a kink. It was not very kinky, as far as kinks go. Even in my limited experience I had knowledge of desires much more forbidden than hers. But, simply put, her fantasy was to be taken roughly in a cheap motel. So I put on my turn signal.

'You're not. Are you?' she asked.

'You don't want to?'

A blush appeared on Angela's cheeks and I parked by the swimming pool.

2.

Angela was too shy to accompany me into the office. The carpet was old, thin, and grey. The room smelled musty, like a used bookstore. The woman behind the counter was surprisingly attractive. She must have been thirty – maybe even over forty – but her red hair was a maze of keratin and I got lost in it.

'Welcome to the Shamrock Motel.' She watched me carefully as I approached.

'We'd like a room.'

'Why are you so hungry?'

'Excuse me?'

'You're a pig. Oink! Oink! Hello, little piggy.'

'Lady, please.'

'Are you a pot-bellied? Maybe a Mulefoot? Oh, no, you are a Mangalica! Hello, little Mangalica. Oink! Oink!'

I've always kept myself fit. Even now, as I'm telling you this, my muscles are thick and my stomach remains flat. Her insults were more misplaced than hurtful. Still, she pissed me off.

'Just give me a room,' was all I said.

The woman looked down. I did too. She'd already put the key to Room 8 on the counter.

3.

The lovemaking between Angela and me was frenetic. Nearing the conclusion, our heads were at the footboard and our feet at the headboard. When I pulled out, we were both impressed by how far I shot; missing her body completely, my spunk landed in a long dewy line on the carpet, farther than I'd ever shot before. We fell asleep quickly, almost instantly, both of us, but I woke up six hours later. Even though the only light in the room was from the street light in the parking lot, I could see everything, and what I saw was shocking.

Nine woman grew like plants from the carpet. They stood close together, but lined up, one right next to the other like a row of corn. I recognized each one: Donna, Penny, Janelle, Jess, Toby, Caitlin, Michelle, and Mikaela. I'd loved them all and I still loved them, or so I believed, as they grew out of the carpet in chronological order. They weren't made of flesh, but some sort of plant material, like sugar cane. They were proportioned perfectly: hips and boobs, the tilt of their noses, the lobes of their ears, all of it was perfect, but tinted green. All their eyes were closed and they swayed as if moving to some music I couldn't hear.

They looked absolutely delicious. The longer I looked, the more hungry I became. Soon I was famished. What could I do but take a bite out of one of them? Promising myself that the bite would be so small that the plant herself wouldn't notice, I got off the bed. Angela continued sleeping. I decided to start with Donna, since she'd been my first. Getting down on my hands and knees, I bit into Donna's stalk. As soon as I did, Donna's eyes opened.

'I'm sorry! So sorry!' I said, although I did not spit out the bite of Donna I'd taken. It was the best-tasting thing I'd ever eaten.

'More! More!' the plant said.

'I promise not to eat any more!' I said as I continued chewing.

'No, eat more of me! Please! Eat all of me!'

I didn't need to be asked twice. I ate more, taking bigger bites, and before I knew it I'd eaten all of Donna. As the last bit of her slid down my throat, I knew it wasn't Donna I'd consumed. It was the last of the love I still had for her. Love I'd been holding on to for years. All of it was gone. I no carried love for Donna Remington inside me.

'Me now!'

'No, me!'

'Me next!'

'Eat me!'

All the plants were pleading to be eaten. Their whispery voices were smooth and rough, like a choir of angels and crows.

'Wait, you mean you *want* me to eat you?' I asked.

'We do ... '

'Yes!'

'Me first!'

'Why?' Looking over my shoulder, I made sure Angela was still asleep.

'We are filled with sadness and sorrow.'

'So painful!'

'What good is love that cannot be expressed? End it!'

'End us!'

'End our sadness and pain!'

They continued like that, getting louder and louder. I was afraid that Angela would wake up and see all of them there, growing out of the carpet. How would I explain that away? What else could I do? I had no other choice. I went from one plant to the next and ate them all up, from stalk to tops. I ate and I ate and I ate. I ate all of them up. And when I'd finished eating the last plant in the last row, all my old love was gone. Whether for Michelle, or Jess, or Penny, or Caitlin, it was all gone. My heart held love only for Angela.

I burped loudly and went to the bed. Angela was sleeping. I shook her.

'Wake up! Wake up!' I told her.

'What? What's wrong?'

'I have my answer.'

'I'm listening.'

Everything was riding on my answer. I had to say the perfect thing. I took my time, organized all my thoughts, and only when I was sure I'd composed the perfect speech did I began to speak.

'Love, once felt, expands outward like the universe, travelling slightly faster than the speed of light,' I said. 'So that when you arrive in the future it's already there. Travelling backwards at the same incredible speed so that it's always existed. Love is a never-ending loop, ending where it begins and beginning where it ends. So, in effect, love never ends.' I could tell from the look in her eyes that it'd worked.

'Yes! Yes! I will marry you!' Angela said.

She held me tightly. She kissed me, deeply, passionately. I turned out the light. I kissed her cheek. I kissed her neck. I kissed her from head to toe and I took only the tiniest little nibbles.

Burt Reynolds

1.

There are six Olympia Tannings sprinkled around the Greater Toronto Area, but the one George frequents is in a strip mall near Etobicoke, a suburb he rarely has any reason to be in. George, a slightly-less-than-middle-aged information security analyst manager at Faber and House, who spends his days in a windowless office surrounded by pasty office workers marinating under fluorescent lights, discovered the location when a stalled vehicle in the left lane of the 401 convinced him to try getting home on the Queensway. When he was stopped at a red light, George's attention was attracted by their sign, a picture of Hercules wearing shades and very little else, and the name stuck in his head for weeks.

He booked a session, even though the Queensway location required a forty-five-minute drive and there was one on Dupont, way closer to his new apartment. This was months ago; he's had lots of time to book with the closer location and yet he never has. George is still driving all the way out to Etobicoke. One day George runs into Stephen in the hallway between the booths and the change room. A tall, extroverted pharmaceutical salesman, Stephen and his partner own the house across the street from the one George's wife still owns. The hallway is narrow. They both wear bathing suits. The lighting is dim, but George still doesn't know where to put his eyes.

'George? What are you doing in a place like this?'

'Great to see you, Stephen.'

'I thought I was never going to see you again. One day your car's in the driveway, the next you're gone! Never to return! The street's not the same without you. How's Nora?'

'You'd know better than me. How's Leo?'

'His mom had to be put into a home. Hit him pretty hard.'

'Sorry to hear that.'

'Yeah. Yeah. But, you know, he's okay. He's the same. We're the same.'

'That's good.'

'I'm proud of you, George.'

'Proud?'

'You could have ridden the good ship *Denial* all the way into the grave. Most couples do. Most men do! But you had the guts to get out. That's impressive.'

Stepping forward, Stephen hugs George. They're similar in height, and the tip of Stephen's penis touches the tip of George's. The contact is brief, separated by two layers of recycled polyamide, but undeniable. When Stephen concludes the hug, George takes a step backwards.

'Do something nicer for yourself,' Stephen says.

'What do you mean?'

'Blow some money on something stupid! Take money you'd spend on your family and blow it on yourself. Celebrate yourself! You're looking great, by the way,' Stephen says, then walks down the dimly lit hallway and ducks into Booth 9, leaving George alone and confused.

2.

There's a zucchini in George's hand when it occurs to him that he no longer has to rent a cottage. This is three days after running into Stephen at Olympic Tanning. Frugality is a quality George holds in high esteem. He doesn't feel like he needs to spend money frivolously, on himself or anybody else. However, now that the divorce is official, Nora can rent whatever cottage she wants, for as many weekends as she wants, and he doesn't have to rent one at all. This would mean he has $2,569 to spend however he wants, on whatever he wants, since that is how much they used to spend renting a cottage on the water, just outside of Picton in Prince Edward County, for one fucking weekend.

The cottage they used to rent wasn't the one George would have chosen. He liked that it was on the water, but it felt more like a house – a mansion, even – than a cottage. Advertised as an 'Executive Cottage,' the place had more rooms than they used, a boathouse they never put a boat in, and a large brick outdoor fireplace with ornate ironwork that made roasting marshmallows feel absurd. Having spent his boyhood summers in uninsulated cabins on the west coast of Gabriola Island, he hated the Executive Cottage. The kids, now teenagers with 'friends,' didn't want to go to the cottage anyway.

Still in the produce department, George pokes through bags of carrots, trying to find the biggest, and thinks about new golf clubs and vintage bottles of wine. The front wheel of his shopping cart sticks, but he perseveres, pushing it further down the aisle, stopping to select three English cucumbers and a bunch of bananas. It's a tricky amount of money to spend frivolously, George thinks as he enters the frozen food section, too small to buy a car or a work of art, but too big to blow on a single meal or a new pair of pants. Pushing past the frozen pizzas, George puts two packages of hot dogs into the cart, impulsively buys a box of corn dogs and another of Popsicles. The front wheel continues sticking as he pushes his cart up to the deli counter, passing whole hams and salamis displayed behind glass. George wonders if it wouldn't be best to make a grand gesture, turn it all into fives and hand some homeless guy an envelope, or leave it in the mailbox of a struggling single mom.

'What can I get you?' The butcher's hands look like sausages.

'Two hot Italian and four bratwurst.'

'Good enough.'

The sausages are wrapped in plastic and George puts them in his cart, then makes his way to the front of the supermarket. The sticky wheel has come unstuck. It's only after he's reached the checkout area, standing third in a line of seven, that he realizes everything in his cart looks like dick.

3.

In the middle of the night, George wakes up from what had been a surprisingly solid sleep.

'Dwayne Barlow!' he says.

The name is so stuck in his memory he's sure he will never forget it again. However, just to be safe he reaches for his phone. The blue light makes him squint as he texts 'Dwayne Barlow' to himself. He's already back asleep before the ding announces that the text to himself has arrived.

4.

George got to know Dwayne Barlow well. He remembers Dwayne offering him lines of coke, lovingly laid out on bathroom countertops, at office parties and conventions and retreats. That he kept a rolled-up hundred-dollar bill, which he'd named Sir Robert, in the inside pocket of his jacket. He worked at George's company for less than a year before getting a better job at a rival organization. Everything else George knows about Dwayne Barlow is shockingly personal, patchwork narratives from end-of-the-evening storytelling exchanges, both of them sniffling like they were running fevers.

George sets up a lunch for the following Wednesday. Arriving early, George discovers that Dwayne is already there. They shake hands as Dwayne continues a call. A waitress brings George a rum and Coke that he hasn't ordered. After some time, Dwayne ends the call.

'George! Jesus, you look great. How are things at Faber and House?' Dwayne finishes his drink, holds up his empty glass so the waitress can see it.

'Pretty much exactly the same. And you? How's Howlstein?'

'I'm at Huronia now. And it's good. Very good!'

George checks his phone in an unsuccessful bid to make himself feel important. The waitress brings him a fresh rum and Coke, which he stirs with his index finger.

'Listen, George. Good to see you and all, but I have to be honest and tell you that I've got another thing lined up at three. Here. Afraid I'm gonna need that seat.'

'Okay?' George checks his watch: three is eight minutes away.

'What can I help you with, George?'

'Well, ah ... there was – I remember you telling me a story about a woman?'

'You're gonna have to be more specific.'

'A professional woman?'

'More specific still.'

'With a particular specialty?'

'George, you're killing me! Spit it out, man!'

'The Burt Reynolds?'

'Peggy? You wanna book Peggy?'

'Yes. That's it.' George is unable to look at anything other than his rum and Coke.

'You dog! I suddenly have so much respect for you! But, my friend, Peggy does not come cheap.'

'More or less than $2,569?'

'That should do it.'

5.

Six days later, George unlocks the door to Room 10 of the Shamrock Motel, turns on the television, then sets a thick envelope in front of it. He takes his second shower of the day. Wearing a towel, he turns off the television. He turns it back on. He's still standing in front of it, looking at his pink toes on the thin grey carpet, when the door opens and there she is, carrying a purse that is very large and purple.

'I'm Peggy,' Sally says.

'I'm Brian.' George realizes it's too late to run away.

'This is for me?' she asks.

'It is.'

'Thank you.'

The envelope is placed inside the large purple purse and Sally carries both into the bathroom. When she comes out she's wearing the same dress, and they lie down on the bed. Things escalate quickly. After he cums, George stays on the bed, staring up at the ceiling, as Sally goes into the bathroom. He decides that's it, that's all he wants, he'll just get dressed and go home. But when Sally comes out of the bathroom, still wearing the same sundress, with a protrusion in the front that George doesn't even notice, she's not having it.

'On all fours.' Her voice is low, authoritative, which George, inside a motel room he'll never return to, where no one knows he is, is able to admit is arousing. He gets on all fours.

'Head down. Ass up.'

He does what Peggy says, looks over his shoulder, and sees her pull the dress over her head. The purple cock strapped to her pelvis is very realistic and significantly larger than he anticipated.

'There's no way that's gonna fit,' he says.

'Trust me. I'm a professional.'

Coconut oil is spread over the length of Sally's purple cock and her index finger. The finger is slipped inside George's ass. A second one follows. Lost to pleasurable sensations, George doesn't realize – or at least he doesn't protest – when he feels the tip of her cock pressing against his well-lubricated ass. He takes a deep breath. Slow progress is made.

'I'm not – ' he whispers.

'Shhhhhhhhh.'

The sounds George begins making surprise him. He's never heard himself make sounds like this. It's not so much painful – although there is pain – as confusing. He can't figure out if it's the mental or physical aspect of penetration that makes every sensation both pleasurable and terrifying. And then, much to his surprise, a portal opens at the foot of the bed. It's the size of a tennis ball and emits a pinkish-green light that becomes bigger in direct proportion to the amount of Sally's cock he takes up his ass. The portal grows to the size of a basketball, then a refrigerator, then gets so big that George is sucked inside.

At first everything is black, then there's a light at the other end, far away, which George walks toward. He walks for hours and reaches a high rocky ledge. Far below is a verdant valley where five hundred men – only men – are doing everything imaginable. Everyone is beautiful, every cock is hard, and they cum easily, in unison, in unbelievable volumes all over each other. Then they find new partners and positions and start all over.

'Welcome to Queertasticland!' The Mayor of Queertasticland wears a red Speedo. The sash across his hairless, well-developed chest reads *Mayor*.

'Who are you?' George asks.

The Mayor of Queertasticland points to his sash. Far below, the moaning builds, louder than a stormy surf, increases in pitch and tempo, and then five hundred men cum in unison.

'Holy fuck!' George says.

'Did you just come through that portal?' the mayor asks.

'Yes?'

'Ohhhhh, baby! Are you taking it up the ass for the first time?'

'Kinda?'

'That's not a kinda question.'

'I'm ... I'm getting pegged?'

'Oh, look at you! What's your name?'

'George.'

'George, it's perfectly natural for you to be confused right now. You're out of your comfort zone. You're trying something new, and confusion's the first stop on that tour. But don't be freaked out. I want you to take a good look down there and tell me what you see.'

'It's ... '

'Gay! Those men are gay! Gay! Gay! Gay! And maybe you are too? Who knows? But much more importantly: Who cares, George? What's really going on down there is that a bunch of human beings are doing what turns them on.

They're expressing themselves, fucking the way they want to fuck, which is a surprisingly difficult thing to do these days.'

'I'm still ... '

'Confused?'

'Ashamed?'

'Let me ask you this, George: Is it turning you on, getting pegged?'

'It ... I mean, yes.'

'So it feels good?'

'It does feel good.'

'Is it hurting anyone? You or anyone else?'

'It isn't.'

'Well, there you go! If you can admit that the things that turn you on are turning you on, you're almost home.'

'Am I?' George looks down at the valley. Just as he spots the path that leads to a staircase and realizes it wouldn't be hard to climb down there and join the group of hot incredibly good-looking men, there's a flash of pinkish-green light; he's pulled backwards, into the tunnel.

'Bye-bye, George! Thank you for visiting. You should really think about trying real cock!'

The portal collapses. George is back on the bed. Sally's cock is almost all the way up his ass.

'You okay?' Sally asks.

'Yup.'

'How's it feeling?'

'Harder. You can go harder now.'

And she does. She goes much harder. And George stops resisting, completely, submits to the pleasure. He takes the length of it. He takes everything Sally has to push forward.

'Do you like it?' Sally asks, continuing to rock back and forth.

'I do.'

'What do you like?'

'Taking it ... '

'Say it.'

'Taking it up the ass.'

'And what does that make you?'

'Alive. Motherfucking alive,' George says, proud of himself, knowing that he has a long way to go and a short time to get there, but he's gonna do things they say can't be done.

The River Season

1.

As a teenager, Marina Porte could descend a staircase with a volume of the *Encyclopaedia Britannica* on her head and now, at thirty-seven, she's an orthodontist with her own practice and assistants and her posture is still perfect. She's proud that she spent all Grade 12 going steady with Robert Goodall before she let him stick it in her and that she's grown up to be the kind of woman who makes the bed the moment her feet touch the floor, does all the laundry and vacuuming without bitching about it, counts calories, and still makes the effort to handwash her bras late at night so they'll be dry by morning and she can pluck them from the shower curtain rod before Doug sees them. She is a woman who always uses utensils, does not like using her fingers for anything – so it seems very out of character, especially to herself, that she's using them to point the plastic stick directly into her own urine stream.

She's doing it in private, in the upstairs bathroom, with the door locked and the house empty. Her black hair is tied back, but her makeup is done, midnight-black eyeliner and scarlet lipstick that's been her trademark since the nineties, wearing the Britney T-shirt she sleeps in, which with nothing on below makes her long legs look bird-like and stupid, she thinks. She's embarrassed! This is embarrassing! It's embarrassing to be this embarrassed about doing something so healthy and normal, something she's wanted for so long. She doesn't want to be sneaking around. She just needs to know before he does. It's her body that'll be doing all the magic. Let's see Doug transform ramen noodles and scrambled eggs into a human fucking being. She keeps peeing, pushing it out, past the seven-to-ten-seconds mark, prolonging the embarrassment to avoid a false result. Finally there's no more in her. By the time she has washed her hands and dressed, way more than the package-recommended minute has gone by.

She can't look. Not yet. So she runs down to the kitchen, finds a zip-lock, and keeps her eyes on the end of the stick as she puts it into the plastic bag, then seals it shut, checks the seal, and wraps the whole thing with toilet paper. Stuffing all of it into her handbag, she rushes out the door. Doug's already in the car, waiting impatiently, drumming the steering wheel and looking at his watch as she hurries down the driveway.

'Sorry that took so long. It's freezing in here.' Marina shuts the passenger door and pulls on her seat belt.

'What were you doing? It's not that cold.'

'Can I turn it down?'

'What were you doing in there?' Doug pulls out of the driveway and accelerates quickly.

'Are we in a rush? Why is it so cold?'

'You find it cold?'

'Can I turn down the AC?'

'I guess?'

‘Thank you?’ She turns it down, but just a bit, not as much as she’d like.

It’s been like this for weeks, talking in questions, fighting about how long to boil potatoes, or if the carpet needs steam-cleaning; weeks since he’d repeatedly texted her that they were finally going to let him play shortstop and she still didn’t go. She stayed in the backyard, drinking coffee and lying in the sun, and that just felt more important in that moment. But then she didn’t go to the next game. Or the game after that. Somehow missing two consecutive games made it impossible for her to attend any of Doug’s games, or even to pick him up after one. When she imagines Doug playing baseball, all she sees is him all alone in the infield, waiting for her arrival, pulling up handfuls of grass and looking like the least-loved child in the world. Why does she have to explain that sitting in the backyard drinking coffee is just as important as his baseball game? Why does she have to keep justifying herself to herself?

The fighting continued, and Doug’s team made the finals. Marina couldn’t take the tension anymore, so she volunteered to go with him, drive all the way to South Hampton, and see the last game of the season.

It’s a three-hour trip each way, which is crazy, but he said he’d drive. They drive all afternoon and it’s almost three when they get lost. She still hasn’t looked at the plastic stick. The game starts at seven. The road is gravel and twisted and neither of them can get cell reception. They’re desperate to find their way back to the main road, when out of nowhere, at the side of the road like a backwater Brigadoon, appears the Shamrock Motel.

‘I’ll fuck your brains out if we blow off your game and get a room,’ Marina says.

‘You’re serious?’

‘I’ll do things you’ve only dreamed of.’

Doug’s moment of hesitation is short enough that he’s already forgiven by the time they’re parked by the swimming pool. Doug goes to get out, but Marina puts her hand on his knee and shakes her head in a determined way.

‘If you insist.’ Doug happily watches her walk across the parking lot, alone.

2.

The carpet is thin and grey and the light is bright enough and at just the right angle to expose the dust in the air. At the counter she tries not to stare and, liking her new feeling of decisiveness, of knowing what she wants and going for it, Marina gets to the point.

‘I’d like a room,’ Marina says.

‘I understand,’ Rosemary says.

‘That I want a room?’

‘That you’re scared. Scared that all your favourite girly bits, the ones you love the most, the ignoble ones, will become not just overshadowed but obliterated. That you’ll be reduced to a uterus. That your purpose in life, the way others see you and you see yourself, will be reduced to a single confining role. That your most private territory is already being redefined, colonized by the expectations of society. Yes?’

'Yes.'

'From the age of ... seventeen?'

'Fourteen.'

'From fourteen you've fucked like a dirty slut but kept it secret. Not that you were sexually active, but how much you loved it. That you loved all the dirty whorish pleasures you weren't supposed to love. You acted passive, pretended ignorance, did what you needed to do to look like the good girl, while inside dark desires kicked against eons of social conditioning. And now you're afraid that your cunt's going legit – that you don't have a cunt, you have a womb, something sacred and thereby enslaved, serving a great magnificent purpose so elevated it comes without material reward.'

A clock ticks. Something large cannonballs into the pool. Marina takes a step back from the counter, her eyes focused on something very far away.

'Something like that?' Rosemary asks.

'Exactly like that.'

'Would you like to use that fear to your advantage?'

'How?'

To answer her question, Rosemary sets a key in the middle of the counter.

3.

They enter Room 1 giggling, holding hands, transformed into teenagers, but when she takes a shower she doesn't invite him in. Having brought her purse with her into the bathroom, Marina unwraps the toilet paper, still can't bring herself to look at the stick, and hides the plastic freezer bag between towels in the towel rack. He showers next, and the fact that their clean bodies lie next to each other on crisp white sheets is unable to melt away the weeks of tension between them. They watch television, and after a while she takes his hand, but it doesn't go any further. When the power goes off, they're already asleep.

Hours later the power comes back on, and the suddenly blaring television wakes them. The lights they've left on shine brightly. Naked and facing each other, they don't say a word, run their hands over each other and start fucking. To Doug it's like his wife's become unhinged; he's not making suggestions but trying to keep up. Leaning forwards and backwards, adjusting position and depth, Marina finally finds it, the mythical spot, and works it, hard. Tension builds and builds, and when it finally breaks, she gushes, something she didn't even know her body could do.

The amount of water that comes out of her surprises Marina. She's even more surprised when it keeps flowing, a steady stream rushing out of her, cascading over the edge of the mattress like a waterfall. Water pools at the foot of the bed, then flows across the thin grey carpet, making several twists and turns before running beneath the credenza and out of sight. She's become a river.

Doug pulls the mattress from the other bed onto the floor, uses the drapes as sails, and makes a mast from the curtain rod. Putting the raft into the river, Doug becomes a sailor.

'I'll be back,' he promises.

'Doubtful.' Marina watches Doug sail away in the mirror on the ceiling. Her husband gets smaller and smaller, then disappears under the credenza that the TV sits on.

Marina watches the river. After some time, tiny creatures appear. They look like dolphins but are covered with blue feathers and have long elegant wings. Smiling octopus-things gather in groups of twelve, join tentacles and twirl in circles, creating water spouts that lift them into the air. Several hours later a new creature crawls out of the river, stands upright, and builds tiny homes on the thin grey carpet. They discover fire, start fishing and worshipping Marina as a god, calling her Riviera, the Source of All Life.

Their villages turn into cities. They overfish, pushing all the other river creatures to near-extinction. As resources dwindle, the shore-things start fighting each other. They sharpen sticks. They invent gunpowder. Eventually they build tiny bombs that explode, leaving plate-sized burn-holes in the carpet, and wipe themselves out. Marina is sad, but then, minutes later, the winged dolphins and twirling octopus-things return to the river in great numbers and she accepts that maybe the shore-things' self-destruction was for the best.

It's a long night. The river keeps flowing out of her. Her husband does not return. The sun has started to rise when she loses faith completely. It's at this moment that Marina spots something at the far end of the river, so far away she can't tell what it is, only that something is moving. The object in question gets closer, and soon Marina recognizes the raft and the lone sailor as her husband. His sails are in tatters. The mast is bent. The mattress barely floats, more under the water than above it. His beard is thick. His arms are sunburnt and his face is blistered. He's lost a lot of weight, is skin and bones. Docking between the queen-sized beds, Doug steps onto the carpet and kneels at Marina's feet.

'I have seen incredible things.' His voice is raspy, and although it's difficult to talk, he continues. 'Trees a thousand feet high with leaves a colour I'd never seen before. Creatures with intelligence far surpassing our own that have created civilizations where science is both religion and love. And yet, witnessing all these wonders made me understand that there is only one truth: that I am nothing without you. I love you. Please, take me back.'

When Doug looks up from the thin grey carpet, Marina's head is raised, watching the river flow out of her in the overhead mirror. Her expression reveals nothing. Several long moments pass, and then Marina looks down at her husband and holds his chin with her hand.

'I will take you back under two conditions,' she says.

'Yes. Thank you. Whatever they are.'

'The first is that our child will be named Riviera.'

'You're pregnant?'

'I am.'

'That's ... amazing!'

'Her name?'

'Riviera. I understand. Riviera.'

'The second is that you must drink the river, all of it, so it will live on inside you.'

'I'd be honoured.'

Kneeling at the foot of the queen-sized bed, his thirst overwhelming, Doug remains still as Riviera tilts her pelvis and wraps her fingers into the hair at the back of his head. Only when he's consumed the entire river is his thirst quenched. They lie on the bed, holding each other tightly and listening to the sound of ice cubes falling inside the ice machine and farm equipment on the gravel road, thinking about all the places the road could lead to, that from this place, given the world they live in, it could take them anywhere.

The Question Most Frequently Asked by Guests of the Shamrock Motel

The question every former guest of the Shamrock Motel asks, although some ask it almost immediately while others don't ask until weeks, years, or even decades after their visit, is this: *So now what*? They've had this crazy experience, possibly profound, potentially life-changing ... and now? As they drive away, gravel pinging the undercarriage of their cars, watching the Shamrock Motel grow smaller in their rear-view mirrors, the euphoria of self-knowledge begins to lose its lustre and a tiny voice in their minds begins to ask practical questions. *Yes, I know myself better, but how does that help me pay for my car? Buy me groceries? Contribute to my RRSP? Can I afford a house? Will I have kids? Find happiness? Will I be happy at all? My husband and I have accepted each other's faults, but will that help me find meaning and purpose? Is there meaning and purpose? What is the point of the Shamrock Motel? Of staying there? Of staying alive?*

Rosemary has also asked these questions repeatedly, especially since the horrible thing happened. She has come up with an answer. She wants you to remember that examining metaphysical things with a rational approach is like looking for the dark with a flashlight. She asks you to think about how unlikely every event of your life is, the unthinkable amount of improbability that had to be overcome to manifest every single moment of it.

Think of everything that had to happen so you could read this sentence. You had to buy, borrow, or steal this book. The printing press, the publishing industry, and storytelling had to be invented. Molecules of oxygen, hydrogen, nitrogen, carbon, calcium, and phosphorus had to arrange themselves in a pattern capable of abstract thought, inventing language, the concept of writing, and the ability to read. Is it really so hard to believe all that happened through something other than random chance? Can it really be a coincidence that you're reading this very book at this very moment?

The owner of the Shamrock Motel urges you to at least entertain the notion that it isn't.

The Credenza

Rosemary bought a credenza off Craigslist, to replace the one in Room 4 that was destroyed when the horrible thing happened, paid extra to have it delivered. A bright white moving van parks beside the swimming pool on August 21, near the end of the day, when the shadows are growing long and the air is finally cooling. She unlocks the door to Room 4, becoming the first person to step onto the new vinyl tiles since they were installed. The air is musty. Her palms are sweating. Rosemary gets out of the way as two bear-like bearded men, stinking of fresh sweat and pride in their work, carry in the credenza and set it against the west wall. She tips the workmen. They leave. Alone in the room, Rosemary opens the credenza's doors and discovers a thirteen-year-old girl inside.

The girl claims to be her daughter.

'Well, isn't that convenient,' Rosemary says.

'What is?' The girl looks quite comfortable inside the credenza. She makes no attempt to get out of it.

'That a thirteen-year-old girl hiding – '

'I'm not hiding.'

'Living?'

'Thank you.'

'That a thirteen-year-old girl living in the credenza I bought on Craigslist would be my biological offspring.'

'That's the way these things work. Don't you know anything?' The girl, her daughter, says these words with such absolute conviction that Rosemary is inclined to believe her. The girl has very long, uncontrollable red hair that Rosemary can't stop staring at.

'Then why don't I remember you?' Rosemary asks, and of course the second that Rosemary voices this question, it all comes flooding back to her: washing Lily in the sink, pushing her in the stroller, her first words, first steps, first day of school.

'Where have you been?' Rosemary, by nature not an overly sentimental woman, can't stop crying. She hugs her child close and tight.

'In the credenza!'

'How did you get in the credenza?'

'You put me in there. Don't you remember?'

'Why would I do such a thing?'

'Because of the horrible thing that happened.' Lily doesn't have to say anything more.

'Okay. I remember that now too.' Rosemary doesn't like talking about the horrible thing that happened. She doesn't even like thinking about it. Nobody does. Not even narrators. It's enough to say that the horrible thing was horrible enough to explain why a mother would stash her daughter in a credenza and suppress all memory of the decision to do such a thing – all memory of having a daughter – just to keep her safe.

'Well, let's get you out of there.'

Rosemary's daughter is surprised by this suggestion. She's been in the credenza for so long she's forgotten that getting out of it is an option. It's dark and cramped and her life inside the credenza is exceedingly boring, yet she is reluctant to leave it. Living inside the credenza has kept her safe during the years after the horrible thing and, as we all know, it's very hard to give up something that makes you feel safe.

'Is it really safe to come out?' Lily asks.

'Yes.'

'Really?'

'As safe as it's ever going to be, sweetie.'

The woman, her mother, says these words with such compassion and sadness that Lily has no choice but to accept their truth.

'Okay.' Lily reaches a tiny hand out of the credenza and Rosemary holds it. She pulls. Getting Lily out of the credenza is not easy. She's grown since going inside the credenza, so it's a very tight fit. Rosemary has to pull and pull. It seems like Lily will never get out, and the more Lily feels like she's stuck, the more she wants out of it.

'Pull harder!' Lily yells.

'I'm trying!' Rosemary yells back. She pulls, harder and harder, and Lily pops out of the credenza, free at least.

The moment she is out of the credenza, she starts growing. In two hours, she's taller than any other kid her age. By midnight, the ceiling of Room 4 is too low. Lily, being tired, decides to go outside and lie in the large grassy area behind the motel.

Gathering blankets and pillows, Rosemary sleeps outside too. Rosemary and her daughter fall asleep together, looking up at stars, but just before midnight the ground begins to shake. Sitting up and looking to the east, Rosemary and Lily see a group of giants, six or seven of them at least, walking toward the Shamrock Motel. Large ripples form on the surface of the pool. Apples fall from the apple tree. The giants are very tall; when Lily stands up, she's taller than the short ones and just slightly shorter than the tallest of them.

The giants talk in a language Rosemary doesn't understand but that Lily is fluent in. Rosemary doesn't know how her daughter learned to speak Giant. It's just one more mystery. Lily and the giants talk for hours and hours, all through the night. When the sun is still below the horizon, but the first hints of pink and purple have crept into the morning light, her daughter steps away from the circle of giants and crouches down to talk to her mother.

Rosemary already knows what Lily is going to say.

'I love you, Mom. I really do. But … '

'I'll miss you.'

'I'm not leaving because of the credenza. Or anything you've done. I want you to know that.'

'I know.'

'I would never have gotten out of the credenza without you!'

'That makes me happy!'

'I know it seems unfair that I'm leaving so soon. After we just got reunited. Able to see each other again. But at least we have this. At least we did get to see each other again.'

'That's true.'

'It helps but it doesn't help?'

'Yes. Exactly. Both.'

They both cry. Lily wraps her hand around her mother's body and squeezes, gently, this being the only way they can hug. Lily stands up and joins the group of giants and they start walking away, holding hands, a long line of giants silhouetted by the rising sun.

'Was I a good mother?' Rosemary calls out.

'You were! The best!'

Rosemary suspects that Lily might just be telling her what she wants to hear, but her daughter says these words with such surprise and conviction that she's forced to accept their truth. She watches Lily and the other giants until she can't see them anymore. And then she stands there a little bit longer. Eventually she goes inside and fills the credenza with all the things her daughter loved most, which are now nothing more than mementos.

'eady and Willing

1.

Just after nine in the morning, on the third Saturday in July, after dropping Christopher at dance class and Lisa at the arena, Melanie Yardwood secretly enters the Municipal Parking Carpark 68 through the St. Andrew Street entrance and drives her grey Subaru past numerous empty spots, up and up, until reaching the open-air roof. The blue sky and seven-storey view remain surprising, slightly magical, a button-downed consequence-free trip through a wardrobe. There are no other cars on the roof of Municipal Parking Carpark 68. In the six Saturday mornings Mel's done this, there has never been another car. It is a fiefdom for her and her alone. Every space is available to her, but Melanie parks by the west wall with the view of the skyscrapers downtown. This is where she always parks.

After rolling down all four windows and killing the engine, Mel reaches under the passenger seat and pulls out a compact disc. The rest of her family doesn't even know the CD player still works. Opening the jewel case, she sees the compact disc briefly reflect the morning sun. The CD player gives a mechanical moan of happiness as it sucks the disc in.

Seconds later, 'Do You Really Want to Hurt Me' by Culture Club plays through the speakers. Melanie increases the volume significantly. The driver's seat is reclined. The song is put on repeat. The third repetition is nearly at its conclusion, and Melanie has begun recovering from her week of carpools, cooking for children, and managing the wealth of other people, when Boy George's plaintive voice is replaced in the speakers by the sound of her phone. The screen in the dashboard displays her husband's name. This happens automatically, beyond her control. If a genie suddenly appeared in the passenger seat, she'd spend all three wishes on acquiring the power to press Decline and ignore his call. But there is no genie in her Subaru, so she pushes the Eject button and the disc slides halfway out, like a toddler's tongue.

She presses Accept.

'Roy? Everything okay?' Mel asks.

'I can't get the cake,' Roy says. A televised crowd cheers in the background.

'Are you watching tennis?'

'You'll have to get the cake.'

'Why?'

'For Dad's birthday?'

'I know: I ordered the cake. And you said you'd pick it up.'

'I did. But I can't.' Roy says nothing more, and the resulting silence is difficult for Mel not to fill.

'Roy. You said – '

'What are you doing that's so important, Mel?'

'I'm ... '

'Exactly. Go get the cake. I'll get a ride with Sarah and we'll meet at Dad's condo.'

‘What about the kids?’

‘Kate’s agreed to pick up the kids.’

‘Your sister?’

‘You know another Kate that would drive across town for you?’

‘No.’

‘Okay?’

‘Okay.’

‘Agreed?’

‘I said okay.’

‘Good.’

Roy ends the call. The driver’s seat is unreclined. Melanie does not push the CD back into the player. Culture Club’s first U.K. #1, which rose to #2 on the U.S. charts, becoming their highest-charting single, is not replayed.

2.

Melanie Yardwood ordered the cake for her father-in-law’s eighty-third birthday several weeks in advance, from an east-end place called Caked-Out, the best bakery in the city, or so she had read. After leaving Municipal Parking Carpark 68, she endures forty-seven minutes of Saturday-afternoon Bloor Street, bumper-to-bumper traffic, parallel-parking cars, pedestrians and bicycles appearing out of thin air, stoplights turning red. But it’s worth it, she thinks, because Elroy Sr. isn’t easy to please and she knows this will please him.

The bakery is housed in a former convenience store. There is no parking. Mel circles the block three times, eventually finding a spot that's barely legal. The sign above the door still says Total Convenience, but the address is right. Inside there's no air-conditioning, a line of six people, and one cashier. An aproned, flour-covered employee carries a tray of doughnuts through a swinging door; even at the back, Melanie can smell them, although the smell has dissipated twenty minutes later, when Mel gets to the front of the line.

'I'm picking up a cake.' Melanie smiles broadly, maybe showing too much teeth.

'For who?' The girl behind the counter is tall and so pale her veins are visible.

'Yardwood.'

'Yardwood?'

'Yes.'

The countergirl slinks into the back and returns empty-handed.

'There's no cake for Yardwood.' Her shoulders scrunch up as she holds her flat empty hands toward the restored tin ceiling.

'Yardwood? Are you sure? You have nothing for Yardwood?'

'Nothing.'

'Can you look again?' Melanie glances over her shoulder, gives the woman behind her an apologetic smile, even though she's not preventing her Jack Russell terrier from sniffing Mel's pant leg.

'There's nothing.' The countergirl tucks her fingers under her armpits, making her hands disappear.

'I ordered it weeks ago.'

'I don't know what to tell you.'

‘Please? I paid in advance when I ordered it, online. Can you just take another look?’

The countergirl sighs Desdemonianly, then disappears through the swinging doors to have a second look. She’s gone for a very long time. The customers behind Melanie tap their toes, give sideways looks, check their phones, performing a symphony of gestures orchestrated to show that they blame Mel for how slowly the line is moving.

It is not my fault they have only a single till open on a Saturday afternoon! Mel wants to say, but doesn’t. *Why bring a dog inside a bakery? If my kid were licking your ankles, I’d have the decency to make them stop!*

Fuck you all!

Mel doesn’t scream any of these things. She doesn’t want to be thought of as a ‘Karen,’ which is now even worse than being a bitch. Although when Mel watches those videos, she often finds herself – not all the time, but sometimes – rooting for the ‘Karen.’ Thinking, *That’s just someone who’s had enough, someone expressing anger and being ridiculed for it because she’s female.* The dog’s breath is back on her ankle, but Mel keeps smiling apologetically, and when the countergirl reappears she’s carrying a white cardboard box, which she passes over the counter. Mel is so pleased she just grabs the box and rushes away, tripping over the terrier, who issues a yelp of pain worthy of a European soccer player.

Mel almost drops the box but manages to untangle her legs and regain her balance. She reaches the door but is unable to look back, knowing that everyone still in line blames *her* for the near-catastrophic accident, not the dog, and especially not the dog’s owner.

3.

Mel takes the parking ticket from under the wiper blade, then puts the cake on the passenger seat and drives west. The traffic is worse. She's never going east of Yonge again. But when her finger pushes the buzzer to her father-in-law's condo, she's only ten minutes behind schedule. Roy buzzes Mel up and meets her at the door.

'Where have you been?' Roy's whisper-scream is louder than his indoor voice, but for the moment Mel can't think about anything but the absence of his beard. The bottom half of his face hasn't been visible in years. It looks so smooth that Mel can't stop herself from running her hand across his cheek. He knocks her palm away.

'This is where I've been.' Mel shoves the cake box at him. They avoid the dining room, going directly into the kitchen.

'Everybody's waiting.' Roy stops at the sink, turns, and crosses his arms.

'You shaved off your beard?'

'Obviously.'

'What made you shave off your beard?'

'We have to get the cake out. They've been waiting forever.'

'Ten minutes?' Mel unboxes the cake, holds it on an angle for Roy to examine.

'It's a birthday party. You need the cake for a birthday party. Otherwise it's just a ... '

'Family gathering?'

'Don't be a smart-ass.'

'Did you bring candles?'

'Christine did.'

Roy leaves the kitchen. Mel is still searching cupboards, hoping to find a suitable plate, when he returns and sets two packs of twelve multicoloured candles on the counter.

'What am I supposed to do with these?' she asks.

'You want me to do it?'

'He's eighty-three.'

'Then use all of them.'

Roy walks away.

In a stroke of inspiration, Mel arranges them on the cake in two groups: eight candles on the left side, three on the right. There's no lighter in the junk drawer, but it's a gas stove so she removes one of the candles, lights it, lights the others with that. Three are still unlit when Roy and all his siblings begin singing 'Happy Birthday.'

Mel doesn't notice the spelling mistake until she's already out of the kitchen. Her hope that no one will notice the error is dashed when her own husband points it out. Just as Mel sets the cake in front of Elroy, the golden candle glow illuminating every wrinkle on his ancient face, Roy steps forward.

'Wait, wait, wait!' Roy waves his hands and shakes his head like a referee negating a goal. When everyone has stopped singing, he points to the cake. 'Happy Bithday?' Roy says. It takes a few seconds, but then everyone gets it.

'What's a bithday?' Denice, Roy's older sister, asks.

'I guess that makes me the bithday boy!' Elroy Sr. says.

'It's from the best bakery in town.'

'*R* you sure about that?' Nora, Roy's second youngest sister, asks.

‘The ve’y best?’ Bonnie, the youngest, asks.

‘I drove across town just to get it.’

‘’eally?’ Nora asks.

‘’ight ac’oss town?’ Roy says, his voice high-toned.

The candles continue burning and everyone falls silent. The joke seems to have run its course, and Mel releases her bite on the inside of her cheek, glad that the worst has passed.

But it hasn’t.

‘Happy Bithday,’ Roy sings.

‘Happy Bithday to you!’ they all sing. They sing the whole song, right from the top, dropping every *r*. All of Roy’s sisters and all of his nieces and nephews – eleven Yardwoods in total – sing, loudly, sniggering, with exaggerated joy, eager to be in on the joke.

‘And many mo’e!’ Roy’s baritone voice, as always, is loud and rich and sure of itself.

4.

They don’t speak on the ride home. Roy goes to bed. Mel watches television until she falls asleep on the couch. He’s gone when she wakes up, and that afternoon she shows up unannounced at his office. He’s on the phone, seems genuinely surprised to see her, then mimes talking with his hand and rolls his eyes. She stands in front of the window. His office is on the sixteenth floor of the Sun Life Tower. The only thing she likes about it is the view. She pinches three brown leaves from the large dieffenbachia in the corner. There’s no garbage can, so she holds the dead leaves in her hand. When Roy hangs up, she sits in the grey chair in front of his brown desk.

'I guess I didn't inherit my mother's green thumb,' Roy says.

'You're overwatering it. Dieffenbachia need to dry out in low light conditions.'

'Duly noted.'

'Can we talk?'

'What do you want me to say?'

'That it's not my fault. That you're sorry. That you shouldn't have made fun of me.'

'I wouldn't have left the store without checking the cake.'

'Okay.' Mel looks out the window, sees people in business clothes typing, a narrow slice of the lake.

'Roy, it comes down to this: I don't feel like this is a partnership.'

'You want to make the decisions?'

'I'd at least like a greater input.'

'I don't think that's true. I think you like it that I take care of things. Take care of you.'

'You think you take care of me?'

'You don't?'

This is where they usually start fighting, but Mel, carrying a cake box of determination, nimbly steps over the leash that runs between her husband and his controlling impulses. She takes several deep breaths, pictures flowing water, then looks him in the eye.

'All I ask, Roy, is this: sometime in the near future, before the summer's over, I'm gonna suggest doing something. Just one thing. And you have to do it. Commit to it. Really do it.'

'Okay. But if I don't enjoy your suggested activity? If I think it's stupid?'

'If you've really committed to it, really done it, then you've proved your point. And if you do enjoy it, if you think it's a good idea, I've proven mine.'

'One thing? Just one thing?'

'Just one thing.'

'It's a deal,' Roy says.

'A deal? Okay. Yes, a deal.' Mel sets the dead leaves on his desk and leaves.

5.

The next three weeks are pretty good – so good that they rent a cottage on Lake Huron for the August long weekend. So good that they convince Kate to take both Christopher and Lisa for all three days. Roy even lets her drive once they're out of the city. Shortly after he's fallen asleep, the phone suggests a shortcut, which Mel decides to take, quickly finding herself far from the 401, travelling down concessions, side roads, and rural routes, loving the green grasses and actual cows, until her phone crashes and won't reboot. The screen remains black no matter how many times she presses both buttons at once.

Mel drives slowly, worried that the gravel will chip the paint and she won't find her way back to the main road before Roy wakes up. And yet, when she sees the sign for the Shamrock Motel, Mel applies the brakes and the turn signal. She parks by the pool. The lack of motion wakes

Roy and he looks around, surprised to see that they're at a motel.

'Where are we?' Roy asks.

'You promised that I could have one thing. And that you'd commit to it.'

'Come on.'

'One thing, Roy. You promised.'

'And you want this to be it?'

'I do.'

The car's interior light goes on in the bright afternoon sun as Melanie gets out of the driver's seat. Roy watches his wife cross the parking lot from the passenger seat, a perspective he is unused to. Wearing his reluctance like a rented tuxedo, Roy exits the passenger seat and goes through the office door that Melanie holds open for him.

'Welcome to the Shamrock Motel!' Rosemary Liszt says.

In an attempt not to stare at the woman's hair, Melanie casts her eyes down to the thin grey carpet, but looking away makes her lose her nerve and now she can't look up. Her neck's immobilized, rusted, her voice mute; she's unable to utter the magic words needed to conjure a room, which is crazy. This is so hot for her. Getting fucked in the middle of the day in a cheap motel room is her go-to fantasy. The ice machine hums and Roy jingles coins in his pocket.

'I can't just give you one,' Rosemary says.

'I don't ... Pardon?' The tops of Mel's shoulders are question marks.

'You have to ask for it. It's kinda the whole point of the Shamrock Motel.'

Melanie looks over her shoulder, sees her husband's sour face, pale as milk, remembers how, three hours earlier, over lunch, she'd imagined plunging a steak knife into the middle of his hand.

'A room then. Yes. We'd like a room,' Mel says.

'Queen or king?'

'King! Can we use cash?'

'It's what we prefer.'

Melanie is not asked to sign a register or present identification. A surprisingly small amount of money changes hands. Rosemary turns and looks at the wall behind the counter, where fourteen keys hang from sixteen hooks. She selects the key to Room 3 and sets it on the counter. Melanie reaches for it, and Rosemary, with a sudden firm movement, traps Melanie's hand against the counter.

'Do you really want it?' Rosemary applies downward pressure. The key digs into Mel's hand.

'I do.' Melanie turns and looks at her husband, who remains by the door, hands in pockets, oblivious.

'Even if it changes everything forever?' Rosemary asks.

'Yes.'

'Are you sure? Those aren't words to be uttered lightly around here.'

'I said yes!'

'What do you really want, Melanie?'

'I want what everyone wants.'

'What's that?'

'To be happy.'

'That's it?'

'I want to ... '

'To?'

'To do what I want.'

'What if what you want isn't what he wants?'

'Why wouldn't it be?'

'Don't act naive.'

'I'll do it anyway. If he really loves me, he'll understand.'

'You think?'

'We've made a deal.'

'Is that all your marriage is? A deal?'

'Let go of my hand.'

'Just tell me what it is that you want right now, Mel. Say it out loud.'

'I want the key!' Mel says, and, using unexpected strength, pulls out her hands and wins custody of the room key.

'Enjoy your stay,' Rosemary says, smiling.

6.

Sixteen minutes later they're lying in bed when the power goes out. Roy is already asleep. Mel gets out of bed wearing the white cotton sheet and a look of unsatisfied longing. She looks out the window. Sunlight sparkles off the pool water. The OPEN sign in the office window is off. The power looks to be off in the whole place.

'You expecting 'ain?' Roy says, smiling, laughing at his own joke, then falls back asleep, his arms and legs sprawling out like suburbia. Melanie could kill, but instead looks back out the window and sees fully formed, fully erect cocks falling from the sky. No men fall from the sky, only cocks, fully formed and erect. Melanie thinks she's dreaming, but after several failed attempts to wake herself, she accepts that she isn't.

Cocks continue falling from the sky, and Melanie steps closer to the window to get a better look. These cocks are gorgeous. Each one is long but not too long, with substantial girth, which is Melanie's favourite type of cock. It's like these cocks were tailor-made for her.

Still tense from unrelieved desire, Mel ties the bedsheet around herself like a toga – something she hasn't done since her freshman year, then opens the door and goes outside. She stands on the sidewalk, protected by the overhang. The number of cocks falling from the sky hasn't slowed down. It is a heavy rain of cocks. She watches them fall, wondering if she should wake her husband, but rejects this idea: he'd just be jealous, or envious, and he'd certainly demand that she come inside immediately and stay away from the window as he pulled the drapes closed. Just imagining his fists curling into balls and his cheeks growing red makes her want to step out from the overhang.

And so she does.

It doesn't take long before the cocks become aware of her presence. They start falling on an angle, aiming for her. The ones that have already landed wiggle over the pavement in her direction. There are so many cocks, all focused on her, that Melanie becomes overwhelmed and starts running, jumping over the cocks on the ground and dodging the ones falling from the sky. Mel runs past the office and around the ice machine and behind the motel. She climbs a short fence and jumps into a verdant meadow. The cocks give chase.

Mel runs as fast as she can, but the cocks are gaining. Ignoring the stitch in her side, she keeps running, but the bedsheet flopping around her legs makes it difficult to go fast. She seldom runs in bare feet, and the yard is full of thistles. There's a second fence, this one made of barbed wire, which will be difficult to climb, although this is not why Melanie stops.

'Why am I running?' Mel asks herself. She cannot deny that she finds the cocks gorgeous. Or that her arousal is high. She drops the bedsheet toga. The sun feels amazing on her ass. Finding a thistle-free spot in the grass, she lies down amongst bedstraw and bellflowers. The cocks form a line. They're excited, but respectful. Melanie nods at the cocks at the front of the line. Three rush toward her and get busy. When their passions are concluded, the next three cocks step up.

Melanie spends the afternoon being fucked by beautiful perfect cocks, three at a time, one in each of her holes. It's dark out when she's fucked the last one. She forgets about the bedsheet and walks out of the field naked, past the ice machine, goes past the windows of Room 1 and Room 2 without shame.

Roy sleeps as Melanie showers and dresses. The car keys are still in her pocket. Her wedding ring is not easily removed, requiring significant strain and several applications of soap. But she gets it off and leaves it on the bedside table beside the room key. Closing the driver-side door, Melanie starts the car and pulls out of the parking lot. Twenty minutes later, when she finds herself back on the highway, Mel lowers the windows and puts her favourite pop song on repeat, listening to it over and over again, never tiring of it, not even a tiny little bit.

Best Friends Forever

1.

One-Hour Cleaners says it'll take three hours. It's already after noon, which means Molly should be three hours north of Toronto, travelling at highway speed toward Sault Ste. Marie. Yet here she is, almost twenty-nine, standing on an unwashed linoleum floor, taking a black dress out of a white plastic grocery bag. The dress is wet from repeated applications of OxiClean, smells like American cigarettes, and is the only thing she can wear to the funeral of her once best friend, Heather Brown. Covered with stains, the dress is as much a scrapbook as an item of clothing: red wine preserved at the hemline, incriminating drops of marinara sauce at the waistline, DNA samples at the neckline.

'But you're named One-Hour Cleaners.' Molly's attempts to remove wrinkles with her hand are ineffective.

'We can have it back by four. Maybe three.' The clerk, Ben, returns his interest to a television at the end of the counter, where portly British men are playing darts.

'There's hardly any fabric to it.'

'If you put it in now, you can have it back at three-thirty. Probably closer to four,' Ben says, looking at the television.

Molly leans forward. Two darts hit green and one goes into the red.

'Can I pay more? For a rush job?'

'You can. But the dress won't get cleaned any faster.'

'Really?'

'Probably closer to four.'

Ben quotes a price. Molly pays with her credit card. The phone in her pocket rings. Nodding at the clerk, Molly goes outside, answers it, holding the phone so tightly her fingers hurt.

'Hey, Mrs. Brown!' Molly says. There's silence. Molly realizes she's being way too chipper.

'Molly?'

'How is everything, Mrs. Brown? How ... how are you holding up?'

'Are you at the airport?'

'No. No. I'm driving.'

'To the airport?'

'No. I'm not flying. I'm driving.'

'What? Molly? Really?'

'I'll be there, don't worry.'

'Can we help? Is there any way we can help?'

'Already on the road.'

'Is it too late to fly? To turn around? We'll buy a ticket for you, Molly – no problem, no questions asked.'

'I'm gonna be there. I am. I'm gonna drive all night if I have to.'

'I just want to say ... everybody wants you here. You know that. And you know how much Heather ... I'm sorry ... I think this is something you'll regret not being at, Molly.'

'I know.'

'Let me look up the next flight.'

'I'm gonna be there. I promise. I'm already on the road,' Molly says. A streetcar passes in front of Molly and the steel brakes squeal before she can mute her phone.

'Okay, Molly. Okay. I hope you're well.' Mrs. Brown hangs up before Molly has a chance to say goodbye.

2.

Molly has never not known Heather Brown. They grew up six houses apart, Heather's house as chaotic and crammed with siblings as Molly's was orderly and empty. Through a combination of necessity and ingenuity, Heather had been the first to discover everything. That abandoned beer bottles found in parks and garbage cans could be turned into money. How a pillow could maximize the feelings provoked by a full-colour photo of Justin Timberlake. That attention wasn't always what you wanted. Heather's boobs came in before anybody else's, prompting a new round of discoveries: that boys would pay to take you to the movies, a certain look older guys gave, and if they did, it was best to steer clear of them completely.

In high school Heather showed Molly how to calculate integers, tapped out iambic pentameter and the magic spot she couldn't believe Molly hadn't discovered on her own. They went to university in Waterloo, Heather fighting the good fight as an engineering student at the University of Waterloo and Molly majoring in music at Wilfrid Laurier.

They shared clothes, secrets, a sequence of apartments, and sometimes Molly's boyfriends.

But that's as far as it ever went. Heather always had her own bedroom, even if she rarely slept in it; nine nights out of ten she'd sneak into Molly's bed and Molly wouldn't object, or advocate, and they'd sleep back-to-back, two feet of empty bed between them.

3.

The Esso gas station is busy, a tidepool of anarchy, so many cars lined up that Molly's back bumper sticks out onto the road. The pumps are accessible from both directions, creating an outlaw situation, drivers becoming self-appointed sheriffs making sure nobody steals their place at the pump. Feeling above this, Molly waits, patiently, claiming her spot only after letting a black Honda Civic cut ahead. She doesn't rush, checks her oil, buys a three-gallon plastic jug of windshield wiper fluid and tops up the reservoir.

As the car behind her honks, Molly goes inside and pays in person. Her card is declined, forcing her to use the dwindling amount of the cash she has on hand. Returning to the pumps, she notices that her right rear tire is a little soft. Maybe? She gets in, starts the engine, circles around to the coin-operated air pump at the back of the lot.

Blocking Molly's path to the air pump is a black Range Rover, an elephant of a car, grille at eye level, the paint shining like taffeta. Molly parks behind it, gets out, has to jump up to see that there's no one behind the wheel. She stretches out the hose, but it will not reach, crosses her arms and looks around but can't pick out the owner. Everyone in her field of vision seems attached to a different car. Standing with hands on hips, Molly waits for six minutes. This feels much longer. Molly's pretty much ready to kill when a middle-aged white woman wearing high heels and dark sunglasses comes out of the kiosk. Keys in hand, she walks toward the Range Rover as if she doesn't notice Molly at all.

'Nice parking job,' Molly says.

The woman presses a button; the doors unlock and the engine starts.

'Would it have killed you to pull just a little bit forward?'

'Ah, sweetie. You having a bad day? Feel the need to spew a little frustration at a stranger?'

'You're lucky I didn't take my keys to it.'

'It's okay that your car is a piece of shit. Everyone's first car is a piece of shit.'

For reasons Molly can't precisely explain, this makes her furious. Her cheeks blush, her breathing becomes short, she blows bull-like bursts through her nose. Molly takes a step toward the Range Rover driver, but the woman fails to react; her high heels remain fixed to the pavement as if they extend three feet into the ground. Molly takes another step, then another, until the two women are so close their eyes can't focus.

The woman hugs Molly. The physical contact is unexpected and jarring, and Molly doesn't twist away. She leans forward, pushing her torso against the stranger's, leaning more and more weight against the woman's perfect posture. Molly cries. Her eyeliner raccoons. As the woman pats the side of Molly's head, she puts her cheek against her chest.

'Is my sorrow real?' Molly asks.

'You're okay. You'll be okay.'

Molly's eyes are closed. They stay closed. The woman lets go, then drives away. When Molly finally opens her eyes, she drives away too, the back tire as soft as it ever was.

4.

After they graduated, Heather got a job at the Bruce Nuclear Plant as a junior electrical engineer and moved to Kincardine, a small town on Lake Huron. Molly stayed in Kitchener. It was the first time they'd ever lived in different towns. Fourteen months after their separation, Molly went to visit Heather. Heather insisted on paying for everything.

'Why don't you just move here?' Heather said. They were watching the sun go down over Lake Huron, which looked like an ocean, pinks and oranges and optimism everywhere.

'What would I do here?'

'Me! You'd do me!'

'What would I do for money?'

'I could float you. Easy.'

If Heather saw Molly as troubled, a fuck-up, it wasn't visible in her expression. Molly knew that she was, though, still a waitress, playing a field that was quickly turning into pasture, that the zenith of her artistic career had come as second oboe/English horn in the Kitchener–Waterloo Symphony, a part-time position that she'd managed to hold for only eight months.

All these things were true. Molly couldn't accept Heather's help. She did not want to be pitied.

'You want me to be a housewife?' Molly said, the tone of her voice mocking, an attempt to use humour as a way of expressing intimacy. Heather smiled sadly, squeezed Molly's hand with her long strong fingers, then let go. Molly didn't know this was the last time she'd talk to Heather.

For the next two and a half years Heather focused on her job as an engineer. On rising up through the ranks at Bruce Nuclear, securing better paying positions with more responsibility. Molly fucked around. Every day she devoted less time to playing scales and practising compositions. Her fingers got thick, her posture rounded, and her expression flattened out. She distracted herself with a sequence of meaningless sexual dalliances. She didn't want meaning. She ran from meaning like a monster under her bed.

And then, three days ago, Heather was T-boned by a black Ford Mustang, adding one last thing to the list of things she'd discovered before Molly: death.

5.

The black dress is waiting when she returns to One-Hour Cleaners. It's on a hanger, wrapped in plastic. Ben holds it carefully, the bottom draped over his arm. The wrinkles are in exile, the stains returned to the people they were plundered from.

'Look good?' he asks.

'Looks great,' she says.

They don't say anything more. He turns the TV back on, and Molly, carrying the dress, rushes away.

6.

She's been driving for an hour, taking whatever shortcuts the phone suggests, rural routes and gravel roads, the firmness of her conviction strong, defiant – then she wakes up behind the wheel with her car racing toward the ditch. Molly steers hard to the left, stomps on the brake, loses control in the loose gravel. The back end swings around, all four wheels sweeping semicircles into the stones. When her car finally stops, it's pointing in the wrong direction on the far side of the road.

Dust settles through the headlights. Her leg cramping, Molly takes her foot off the brake and the car moves forward, slowly. It's still in gear. A seven-point turn is performed. Her hands shake as the adrenaline leaves her body. She drives slowly, tentatively, keeping thirty kilometres below the limit as if the accident sprained her ability to drive. Her sister is right, about everything, about her being a fuck-up, about how she fucks everything up, and her thoughts become a downward spiral about how she's a fucking fuck-up – then the darkness on the right side of her car bursts into light and colour.

Green and pink shine from a pulsating neon shamrock. Bright white floodlamps at the top of poles illuminate a swimming pool. The Christmas lights strung above a parking lot as an inexpensive attempt to create atmosphere emit a warm lighthouse glow. It is not a hard decision to make.

Turning left, Molly parks beside the swimming pool, walks away from the car like a survivor from a plane crash. Taking the dress with her, carrying it over her arms like a wounded pet, she goes into the office and walks across the thin grey carpet toward the red-headed woman behind the counter.

'Have you been driving long?' Rosemary asks.

'Yes.'

'And you have a long way to go?'

'Yes.' Molly doesn't know what to say next. The light bulbs emit an electrical hum. Far away a dog barks a territorial bark.

'I can't just give you one,' Rosemary says.

'One?'

'You have to ask for a room.'

'That's a little weird.'

'Welcome to the Shamrock.'

'Can I pay with cash?'

'It's what we prefer.'

'Then, may I have a room please?'

'You may.'

'How much is it?'

'If you can name ten things you're tired of, I'll let you have a room for free.'

'What?'

'You heard me.'

'Seriously?'

'Yes.'

'That would really help me out.'

'So do it.' Rosemary turns around, takes the key for Room 11 from the wall, and sets it on the counter. The bulbs still hum, but the dog is no longer barking, and Molly still carries the dress in both hands. She looks up from the carpet and takes a deep breath.

'Failing. Fighting. Losing. Wanting. Rent. Aspirations. Obligations. Expectations – those I'm unable to meet. Entropy. And ... '

'Just one more ... '

'Life?'

Rosemary nods, then pushes the key closer to Molly.

7.

The only thing Molly carries into Room 11 is the black dress. She looks for a place to put it, goes into the bathroom, and hangs the dress on the shower curtain rod. She holds it out, looks at it, realizes the dress is everything she wants to be and isn't: sophisticated, simple, and well cared for. Returning to the main room, she sits on the queen-sized bed.

Remaining stressed, needing to sleep and finding herself alone in a motel room, Molly decides to get off. She turns on the television and finds a talk show because sometimes it helps if she can pretend someone is watching. Clothes removed, she lies face down on the bedspread. Multiple scenarios flash through her mind, but nothing clicks. Frustrated, she flips onto her back. This is when five hands rise out of the mattress.

Each hand is female, long strong fingers. Their nails are well-manicured and painted a dark red that she recognizes as Revlon Blackberry. Two of the hands grab her wrists, two her ankles, and one covers her mouth. The more Molly struggles, the tighter they hold her. A pinkish-green light leaks from the gap between the bathroom door and the carpet, and a group of tiny old women – there must be hundreds of them – crawl through it.

The miniature women walk across the thin grey carpet with purpose. They wear blue coveralls and their hair is tied back with bright red kerchiefs, like the women who worked in factories while the men were away fighting the Second World War. They carry lunch buckets and industrial equipment. The tiny women leading the way work in two-person teams, holding extension ladders. When they reach the bed, the ladders are extended and all the women climb onto the mattress. Molly, who doesn't want to have hundreds of tiny women on her, twists her upper body and kicks her legs, but she cannot break free.

Lifting her head, Molly sees the minuscule women sitting in groups of five or six across her body, from her ankles to her neck. Their lunchboxes are open. Most eat sandwiches. Some drink soup from plaid Thermoses, using the lids as cups. They don't seem in a hurry. Eventually, they wipe their tiny faces with even smaller napkins and pack up. Splitting into four groups, they attend to their tools, then get to work.

The first group of miniature women travels to Molly's pubic hair. They hold tiny garden shears and push tiny push mowers. They work Molly's pubic hair like it's the garden of a queen. It's hard going. The hair is thick and hasn't been trimmed in some time. The tiny women take breaks, wipe perspiration from their brows, then get back to work.

The second group carry tiny oxy-acetylene tanks over to the broad part of Molly's right hip, straight to the bleeding-rose tattoo that she's always regretted getting. The miniature women pull down tiny visors and twiddle valves, finding the right mix of oxygen and acetylene. Sparks turn into blue flames, and the tiny women begin removing Molly's tattoo.

The third group of tiny woman descend to her crotch. The hands holding her ankles spread her legs. The women go in with mops. They get into every nook and cranny of her labia majora. Her labia minora are stretched out like curtains and the tiny women clean both sides.

At first Molly just thinks that they're cleaning, that they're eliminating dirt, but then she sees that they're removing a shiny layer of transparent something covering her most intimate parts like shellac. Molly keeps watching; it doesn't take her long to realize that this substance is shame. Using small motions and even smaller cloths, the miniature women work industriously and remove the thin covering of shame from all her bits. They wash her clitoral hood and then, very, very carefully, her clitoris.

It takes a very long time to remove all the shame from her clitoris. Molly comes close to cumming several times.

The fourth group of women stand in a circle by her left ankle, talking amongst themselves and chain-smoking. The tallest looks at her watch and nods. They all put on miner's helmets and turn on the lights. The beams are bright. Carrying big black duffle bags over their shoulders, they approach Molly's vulva and, gently parting the labia, push their way inside.

Molly doesn't know what they're doing in there, or what's inside the black bags, but she can feel them. They stay mainly in her vagina, although several have reached her cervix. Whatever it is that the tiny women are doing in there, it feels more medicinal than sexual.

This soon changes. Molly becomes aroused. Her pelvis thrusts up and down. The tiny women working on the rest of her body set down their industrial equipment and hold on for dear life. Molly's chest rises and falls as her breathing deepens, and a rosy glow rises onto her cheeks. The hands holding her wrists and ankles strengthen their grip while the hand covering Molly's mouth lets go and, triggered by the sudden ability to express herself, she cums.

While recovering, Molly looks down and sees something coming out of her. It's pink, roundish, and translucent. She cannot identify what it is. It moves slowly and seems material and immaterial at the same time. Only when the amorphous pink blob is all the way out and has begun floating upward like a soap bubble, does Molly realize it's her sorrow.

At first she thinks that the amorphous pink blob contains only the sorrows provoked by her failed sexual encounters. This includes her time with Heather, which is easy to pick out since it's the largest. But as the pink blob rises higher, Molly sees that it's filled with numerous sorrows, different kinds of sorrow, her failures and regrets, sins of omission, that the whole pink thing is filled with all the sorrows unavoidably accumulated from living in a world where nothing is certain or fair.

What Molly doesn't know is why she's stored all her sorrow inside her vagina. It doesn't seem like a good place to keep it.

Although, at the same time, it kinda makes sense.

The amorphous pink blob drifts upward, hits the white stucco ceiling, and pops. Sorrow shoots outward, in all directions at once, like fireworks coloured maroon, dark purple, and brown. Molly feels peaceful and optimistic. She savours these feelings, rightfully suspecting that new sorrows will begin accumulating almost immediately. When she looks back at the tiny industrious women, they've started packing up their gear. Gardening shears are cleaned and sharpened. Mops are wrung out. The oxy-acetylene tanks are fiddled with. The women in the miner's caps stand on their own, smoking, not doing anything industrious at all. The large black bags rest on the bedspread beside them, already zipped up tight, their contents hidden away.

When all the tools have been cleaned and packed, the tiny women climb down the ladders, walk across the thin grey carpet, and disappear under the gap at the bottom of the bathroom door. One tiny old woman trails behind everyone else. She doesn't turn her head or wave goodbye, and when she disappears through the gap under the bathroom door, the pinkish-green light disappears too. The hands holding Molly fade away.

Molly remains perfectly still. Several moments pass. Then, moving quickly, she goes into the bathroom and retrieves the black dress. Leaving the key on the bed, Molly carefully carries the dress to her car, delicately hangs it on the hook in the back seat, and carefully drives away. If she drives all night, stopping only for gas, she'll make it in time for the service.

Sun-Kissed

1.

The room is filled with things that don't belong together. There's a dark-wood hutch that's too large for the white-walled clinical room. Lush blue velvet drapes hang down and a little bit onto the grey LVT flooring chosen for cleanability and durability. Leo Teeswater and Stephen Needham, both fit and tanned and in their very late thirties, watch a seventy-eight-year-old woman whose waxy skin looks processed. It's Leo's mother in the bed. Stephen's has already passed. Leo shifts his long legs, crosses his feet at the ankles, revealing yellow-and-green argyle socks. Stephen hates Leo's socks, finds them showy but not showy enough – bold, but in an easy way – then judges himself for judging Leo.

'Should we go?' Stephen asks.

'Do you want to wait in the car?' Leo asks.

'What does that mean?' Stephen is tempted to go wait in the car just to prove a point, but he's unsure what point he'd be proving. If Leo's mother continues sleeping for another six minutes, a full hour will have passed, and Leo will let them leave. That's how it works. Stephen takes Leo's hand; Leo squeezes lightly, but lets it go. All three remain quiet.

'Why don't you just tell her?' Stephen says.

'She's sleeping.'

'Exactly. That'll make it easier.'

'Be serious. This is serious.'

'It's not for her. It's for you.'

'You're not helping.'

'If you don't, I will.'

'Why are you doing this?'

'Mrs. Waters? Jessica? It's Stephen, Leo's partner. He's right here. There's something he wants to tell you.' Stephen leans forward and puts his hands on the bed's metal railing.

'Don't do this.' Leo's voice lacks patience and humour.

'I know some part of you can hear me, Mrs. Waters. He just wants you to know ... '

'Seriously?'

' ... that he's a big fat queer.'

'Jesus!'

'Goes up the down staircase. Limp of wrist.'

'That's enough.'

'You say it. Trust me, it will feel good.'

Leo doesn't say it – he doesn't say anything. They both sit there, saying nothing. Six minutes later Leo stands up and leaves the room and Stephen is left there, sitting all alone.

2.

On the way home from Owen Sound, where Leo grew up and his mother's nursing home is, Leo decides to take back-roads. He says it's so that they can enjoy the scenery. Stephen knows it's so they can argue, that Leo can't fight traffic and him at the same time.

'Moving to a small town won't fix our marriage,' Stephen says, a pre-emptive strike.

It's long been the plan to move out of the city and buy something ramshackle and Victorian in one of the small towns dotting Southwestern Ontario like a childhood disease. Leo's plan anyway. Having grown up in a small town, Paisley, Stephen's not so sure, understands that synonyms of *quaint* include *traditional*, *conversative*, *judgmental*, and *prone to violence*. But then, Leo grew up in a small town too. So why can't he see this? That even if they found a unicorn village, they'd never be anything more than the gay couple; Stephen would always just be Leo's husband. But Leo's been talking about making the move for years, and they've been actively looking for a house for over a year. Although they haven't gone to see a listing in at least three months. Maybe more. Maybe it's nothing. Stephen does enjoy having his weekends free to do what he wants to, but he can't help thinking about the implication of no longer making future plans.

'Fix? Like our marriage is broken?' Leo asks.

'We'd just fight about different things. Wall colours and kitchen tiles instead of laundry and car payments.'

'Like we're a dishwasher? Like we could just call in a repairman?' Leo keeps his eyes on the road. The car gains speed. The tires slip on the gravel.

'Slow down,' Stephen says.

'I can't believe you said that to her.'

'She was sleeping! You said so yourself. Will you slow down?'

‘Relax.’

‘Please.’

‘Don’t be such a ... nervous Nelly.’ Leo does not slow down. Gravel hits the Honda Civic’s undercarriage, hard atonal plunks.

‘Please slow down!’ Stephen’s grip on the door handle tightens.

‘Nervous Nelly!’

‘I really need you to slow down.’

‘Just enjoy a thrill for once in your life.’ Gritting his teeth, Leo makes the car go a little faster. The gravel hits the bottom harder.

‘Please slow down.’

‘Or, you know, trust that I can drive?’ Leo’s eyes remain on the road.

‘Slow down or let me out.’

‘The worst thing that could happen is not always gonna happen. You know that, right?’

‘Let me out!’

The car stops abruptly. The engine continues running. Leo leans over Stephen, opens the passenger door. They do not look at each other. Several moments pass. Dust from the gravel road drifts onto the wildflowers in the ditch, Queen Anne’s lace and knapweed.

Stephen undoes his seat belt, gets out, stands on the road. The passenger door is closed from the inside. Leo drives away. The car goes over a hill. Stephen listens to the sound of their car on the other side of the hill. At the bottom it slides in gravel as it stops. The engine whines as Leo makes a five-point turn and starts heading back. Just before their car gets over the hill, Stephen runs through the ditch and into a cornfield.

3.

Stephen walks through cornfields, pastures, and stands of trees, trying to keep in a straight line, crossing every side road he comes to and avoiding every farmhouse. It's a game to him, Keep Away with himself as the object, until the sun sets. His cellphone has no reception. He gets tired and hungry. He thought it was impossible to get lost in Southwestern Ontario, but here he is, not knowing which way is north, unable to find a farmhouse.

Stumbling across an abandoned gravel pit, Stephen climbs the far side, hoping to get his bearings. At the top all he sees is farmland. The clouds are low. He stands there for a long time, hoping with fairy-tale logic that if he stays perfectly still he'll see their car's headlights. He doesn't, but then, in the distance, low clouds suddenly reflect a pinkish-green glow, like someone has thrown a switch, coloured light appearing out of nothing.

Since it's all he has to go by, Stephen walks toward this strange new light, down the far side of the former gravel pit, into and out of the trees, his head swivelling up and down, finding his footing, then looking back up to make sure he's still going toward the coloured light. The corn rows work in his favour, and on the other side of the field there's a road. On the other side of the road is the Shamrock Motel, the neon sign the source of the light. Seeing the motel makes Stephen happy in a way that seeing Leo should but no longer does.

The day's heat rises from the pavement as Stephen walks across the parking lot. The carpet inside the office is short and grey. Overhead lighting buzzes as he approaches the counter.

'Welcome to the Shamrock,' Rosemary says.

'Your hair is amazing.'

'Thank you.'

'I'd like a room.'

'We can do that.' Rosemary reaches behind her, takes the key for Room 15, and sets it on the counter. Stephen picks it up, then puts a surprisingly small amount of money on his Visa.

'You're not suspicious? That I've arrived without luggage? Or even a car?'

'Sweetie, you're not even in the top five of the strangest things I've seen today,' Rosemary says. She smiles at Stephen and Stephen smiles back. Taking the key, he leaves the office.

4.

Inside Room 15, overtired and unable to sleep, Stephen sits on the edge of the bed, flipping channels, failing to be entertained or even distracted. He has a shower, and when he pulls back the shower curtain, the bathroom is a sauna. Standing in front of the steamed-over mirror, naked, he uses his index finger to write the things he could have said.

I'm sorry.

I take you for granted.

I will do better.

There are others, but he's unable to write them down, even in condensation. Finding a white terry-cloth robe behind the bathroom door, Stephen puts it on, dries his hair with a towel, and goes into the main room, where he's surprised to find Leo sitting on the bed, smiling triumphantly.

'Found you!' Leo says. They embrace, kiss, and Stephen tries to pretend that seeing him feels like seeing the sign.

'How?' Stephen asks.

'I've been driving around for hours! Panicked! Kept thinking about you being alone in the woods. Not good. But when I drove by this place, I just knew you'd be here. The lady at the desk gave me a key. It was like she was expecting me. Did you tell her I was coming?'

'What does it matter?'

They start going at it, make-up sex being one of their specialties. The old bed shakes, the headboard clapping against the wall like applause. Stephen is behind, doggy-style. His eyes are closed, although this isn't the only reason he doesn't notice the top half of his husband separating from the bottom. The split occurs just above Leo's belly button. There's no blood or dangling organs. Leo doesn't feel any pain or discomfort and continues feeling everything happening to both the upper and lower parts of his body.

Still, Leo finds being in two halves disconcerting.

'Stephen?' he calls.

Stephen continues failing to notice that Leo is in two halves. The vigorousness of Stephen's thrusting endures. The top half of Leo's body is pushed closer to the edge of the bed.

'Stephen! Hey! Stephen? Stevie?'

Lost to pleasure, Stephen just keeps going as the top half of Leo's body inches closer and closer to the edge of the bed. Leo tries to grab hold of the headboard: it's out of reach. His grip on the sheets doesn't save him and he falls out of bed — or at least the top half of him does. Covering his head with his hands lessens the impact, but he's not happy. Lying on the floor looking upward, he watches Stephen fuck the lower half of his body.

'Jesus! George! You're amazing!' Stephen yells.

Leo's name obviously isn't George. All Leo can do is wait for Stephen to finish. Eventually, Stephen rolls off and lies on his back, looking up at the stucco, trying to catch his breath.

'Ah ... Stephen?'

'Just ... a sec ... '

'Stephen!'

'Let me ... let me ... just ... ' Stephen starts snoring. Leo makes several attempts to pull himself off the thin grey carpet. All are unsuccessful. Giving up, he lies on the floor looking at Stephen's feet, which stick over the end of the bed and need scrubbing. Stephen continues sleeping. Leo lies on the thin grey carpet. Or at least the top half of him does.

5.

As he lies on the floor, Leo has a lot of time to think. He makes several decisions. It's the middle of the night when Stephen wakes up to pee and finds only the bottom half of his lover with him in bed.

'Leo?' Stephen asks.

'Down here.'

'How long have you been down there? I'm so sorry!'

'Just help me up.'

Leo is easily put back together: when Stephen places the top half and the bottom half next to each other they snap together like magnets. The relationship will not be so easily repaired. Fully reattached, Leo rolls off the bed and jogs around the room, lifting his knees high. He stands in the middle of the room, naked, feeling a kind of glory in his cock.

Leo looks down. Stephen looks at it. They're both amazed as Leo's cock sprouts blue feathers and his balls turn into long elegant wings.

'Please don't leave me,' Stephen says.

'People think true love lasts forever,' says Leo. 'Which means if their love ends, they think it wasn't true. But love, like flowers, happens in two varieties: annuals and perennials. Our love is an annual. Which isn't lesser. We were like a sunflower. Nobody thinks sunflowers are less beautiful than peonies because they only last a single summer. Take care, Stephen. I won't need the car anymore, so you can have it.' Feathers flutter as Leo flies over the thin grey carpet. He hovers like a bee at the door. He dips down so he can reach the doorknob, opens the door, which allows a cool breeze in, and then flies away.

6.

Stephen sits on the edge of the bed in a white terry-cloth bathrobe, staring at his empty hands. The light in Room 15 turns purple, then disappears. He spends the first hour in the dark. The second is devoted to having a second shower, then sitting in the dark, letting the water evaporate from his skin. The next three hours are lost, then he watches network television until a pink light comes through the window like technicolor hope.

Stephen has survived his first night alone. To celebrate, he goes outside to watch the sun rise. The loungers are more comfortable than they look. The pool heater hums. The white terry-cloth bathrobe falls open, exposing his cock to the rising sun, which has just cleared the trees.

'Does that feel good?' the Sun asks.

'It does.' Stephen is only slightly surprised that the Sun can talk.

'Would you like me to keep going?' the Sun asks.

'Sure,' Stephen says.

'Can I hear a *please*?'

'Um, please?' Stephen is not surprised that the Sun's a bit of a control freak.

'Please what?'

'Sir?'

'Please what, sir?'

'Please keep touching my cock, sir.'

'That's better.' The Sun's all over him. Stephen gets hard. He's never been bigger.

'Can I fuck you?' the Sun asks.

Stephen hesitates, briefly. Rolling onto his stomach, he pulls up the robe.

'You have to say it.' The Sun's voice is full of demands.

'Please?'

'Please what?'

'Please fuck me, sir.'

'Where?'

'My ass. Please, sir, fuck my ass.'

'If that's what you want.'

The Sun pushes inside, filling Stephen with a warm pink glow. It's unbelievable! The pleasure he's feeling isn't the result of friction or penetration – it's all about the warm pink glow. It's about sunniness, like he's being fucked by optimism, by a deep and unexpected belief that everything will be okay. The harder the Sun fucks Stephen, the warmer the pink glow gets and the more optimistic he feels. To his great surprise, Stephen is close to cumming, something that never happens through penetration – nevertheless, here it is.

'Fuck! That was fabulous,' the Sun says.

'You were fabulous!' Flipping onto his back, Stephen sees the Sun rising higher in the sky.

'You are amazing!' the Sun calls down.

'No, you're amazing!'

The Sun gets higher. The plastic lounger is cool. The warm pink optimistic glow stays with Stephen and he doesn't want to lose this feeling, this change, this humbling and empowering glow.

7.

Rosemary continues not looking at the clock as the office door opens and the guest from Room 15 walks in. His face is sunburnt. His arms and hands are sunburnt. The white terry-cloth robe is loosely tied and all bits of flesh accidently revealed are sunburnt. The man, pretty much from head to toe, is lobster red, and yet he looks happy, ecstatic.

As Stephen heads toward the counter, he walks past the clock. Rosemary looks at her hands, but her gaze isn't averted quickly enough. Without wanting to, she's seen the clock, and her mind runs the calculation before she can stop it.

The time is 7:38. Bonnie checked out of Room 12 at 6:55. The room has been vacant for forty-five minutes, just two minutes short of the longest time it has gone unoccupied.

It's been an eventful day at the Shamrock Motel. Even rated on a scale calibrated for the Shamrock Motel, it's been a day. Not just for the guests, but for Rosemary too. When she woke up this morning, she didn't know that she'd enter Room 4 for the first time in three years. That she'd reunite with her daughter and then see her go off into the world. And now, as the clock continues ticking, Rosemary fears that today is the day she loses faith.

'Can you help me?' Stephen asks.

'What you need is aloe vera, but I'm afraid we don't have any.'

'What? Okay, but that's not what I need.'

'Are you sure?'

'I need somewhere to ... a place to ... percolate? Marinate?'

'Interesting.'

'I've learned new things. I need to stay somewhere I can just be still and quiet, so I don't scare them away.'

'You'd like to spend an extra night?'

'I'm gonna need more than that. I was wondering if you rent rooms on a long-term basis?'

'Only one.' Rosemary surprises even herself by keeping her voice calm and cool.

'Is it ... ?'

'You're in luck. It's just become available.'

The key for Room 12 is already on the counter, right where Bonnie left it. Rosemary pushes it a little bit closer to Stephen, who picks it up with a sunburnt hand. They nod at each other. When the office door closes, Rosemary looks at the clock. She isn't really so surprised, although greatly relieved, to see that Room 12 has been vacant for only forty-six minutes.

Acknowledgements

Thanks to ...

Alana Wilcox, Russell Smith, Frida Kaufman, Carl Knudsen, Skippy, Tim Brown, Stephanie Domet, James Lindsay and Crystal Sikma, Mike O'Connell and Karri North, Liz Kaufman, Heather McLennan, Rosemary Wagner, the Canada Council and the Ontario Arts Council for continuing to exist, and Shannon for the hair, pretending plot shape and characterization are interesting, and all the everything.

Andrew Kaufman splits his time between downtown Toronto and the shores of Lake Huron. His work, including the cult-favourite novel *All My Friends Are Superheroes*, has won the Relit Award, been nominated for the Leacock Medal for Humour, and been listed among the best books of the year by the *Globe and Mail*. He works part-time at the Epiphany Detective Agency and in the office of the Shamrock Motel.

Typeset in Baskerville Pro, Antique Olive, Las Vegas, and Knockout.

Printed at the Coach House on bpNichol Lane in Toronto, Ontario, on Zephyr Antique Laid paper, which was manufactured, acid-free, in Saint-Jérôme, Quebec, from second-growth forests. This book was printed with vegetable-based ink on a 1973 Heidelberg KORD offset litho press. Its pages were folded on a Baumfolder, gathered by hand, bound on a Sulby Auto-Minabinda, and trimmed on a Polar single-knife cutter.

Coach House is located in Toronto, which is on the traditional territory of many nations, including the Mississaugas of the Credit, the Anishnabeg, the Chippewa, the Haudenosaunee, and the Wendat peoples, and is now home to many diverse First Nations, Inuit, and Métis peoples. We acknowledge that Toronto is covered by Treaty 13 with the Mississaugas of the Credit. We are grateful to live and work on this land.

Edited by Alana Wilcox
Cover design by Ingrid Paulson
Interior design by Crystal Sikma
Author photo by Heather Morton

Coach House Books
80 bpNichol Lane
Toronto ON M5S 3J4
Canada

mail@chbooks.com
www.chbooks.com

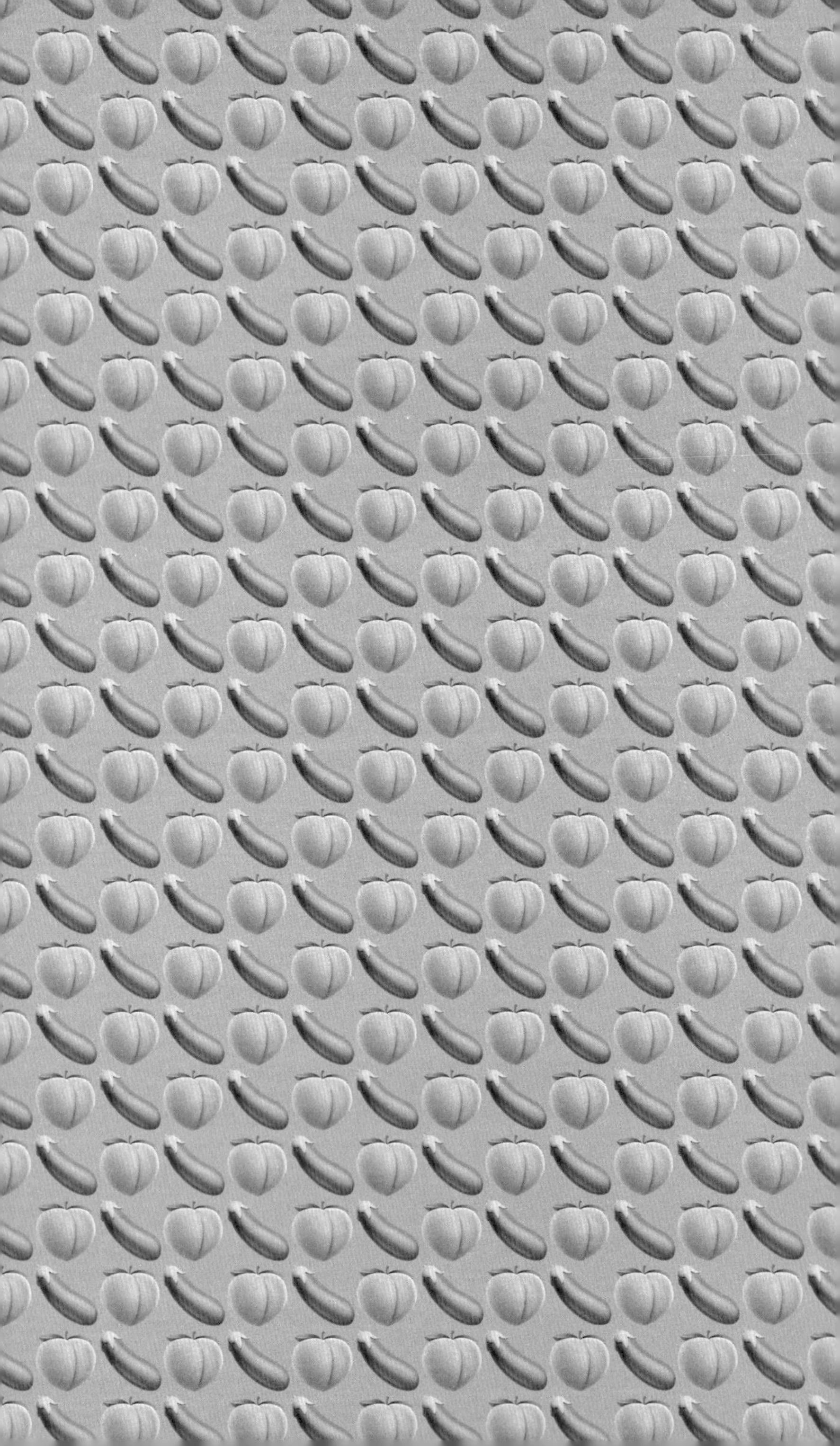